THE ACTUAL TRUE STORY

OF AHMED AND ZARGA

MODERN African Writing

from Ohio University Press
Laura T. Murphy and Ainehi Edoro, Series Editors

This series brings the best African writing to an international audience. These groundbreaking novels, memoirs, and other literary works showcase the most talented writers of the African continent. The series also features works of significant historical and literary value translated into English for the first time. Moderately priced, the books chosen for the series are well crafted, original, and ideally suited for African studies classes, world literature classes, or any reader looking for compelling voices of diverse African perspectives.

Welcome to Our Hillbrow
A Novel of Postapartheid South Africa
Phaswane Mpe
ISBN: 978-0-8214-1962-5

Dog Eat Dog
Niq Mhlongo
ISBN: 978-0-8214-1994-6

After Tears
Niq Mhlongo
ISBN: 978-0-8214-1984-7

From Sleep Unbound
Andrée Chedid
ISBN: 978-0-8040-0837-2

On Black Sisters Street
Chika Unigwe
ISBN: 978-0-8214-1992-2

Paper Sons and Daughters
Growing Up Chinese in South Africa
Ufrieda Ho
ISBN: 978-0-8214-2020-1

The Conscript
A Novel of Libya's Anticolonial War
Gebreyesus Hailu
ISBN: 978-0-8214-2023-2

Thirteen Cents
K. Sello Duiker
ISBN: 978-0-8214-2036-2

Sacred River
Syl Cheney-Coker
ISBN: 978-0-8214-2056-0 (hardcover)
978-0-8214-2137-6 (paperback)

491 Days: Prisoner Number 1323/69
Winnie Madikizela-Mandela
ISBN: 978-0-8214-2102-4 (hardcover)
978-0-8214-2101-7 (paperback)

The Hairdresser of Harare
Tendai Huchu
ISBN: 978-0-8214-2162-8 (hardcover)
978-0-8214-2163-5 (paperback)

Mrs. Shaw
Mukoma Wa Ngugi
ISBN: 978-0-8214-2143-7

The Maestro, the Magistrate &
the Mathematician
Tendai Huchu
ISBN: 978-0-8214-2205-2 (hardcover)
978-0-8214-2206-9 (paperback)

Tales of the Metric System
Imraan Coovadia
ISBN: 978-0-8214-2225-0 (hardcover)
978-0-8214-2226-7 (paperback)

The Extinction of Menai
Chuma Nwokolo
ISBN: 978-0-8214-2298-4

The Wolf at Number 4
Ayo Tamakloe-Garr
ISBN: 978-0-8214-2354-7 (hardcover)
978-0-8214-2355-4 (paperback)

Staging the Amistad
Matthew J. Christensen, ed.
ISBN   978-0-8214-2360-8 (hardcover)
978-0-8214-2361-5 (paperback)

The Cape Cod Bicycle Wars and Other Stories
Billy Kahora
ISBN 978-0-8214-2416-2 (paperback)

The Actual True Story of Ahmed and Zarga
Mohamedou Ould Slahi
ISBN 978-0-8214-2438-4 (paperback)

MOHAMEDOU OULD SLAHI
WITH LARRY SIEMS

THE ACTUAL TRUE STORY OF
AHMED & ZARGA

A NOVEL

with glossary and note on sources

OHIO UNIVERSITY PRESS ▪ ATHENS

Ohio University Press, Athens, Ohio 45701
ohioswallow.com
© 2021 by Mohamedou Ould Slahi

To obtain permission to quote, reprint, or otherwise reproduce or
distribute material from Ohio University Press publications,
please contact our rights and permissions department at
(740) 593-1154 or (740) 593-4536 (fax).

Printed in the United States of America
Ohio University Press books are printed on acid-free paper ⊗ ™

31 30 29 28 27 26 25 24 23 22 21   5 4 3 2 1

Library of Congress Cataloging-in-Publication Data
Names: Slahi, Mohamedou Ould, author. | Siems, Larry, author.
Title: The actual true story of Ahmed and Zarga : a novel / Mohamedou
  Ould Slahi, with Larry Siems.
Other titles: Modern African writing.
Description: Athens : Ohio University Press, 2021. | Series: Modern African
  writing
Identifiers: LCCN 2020043047 (print) | LCCN 2020043048 (ebook) | ISBN
  9780821424384 (paperback) | ISBN 9780821447307 (pdf)
Subjects: LCSH: Bedouins—Mauritania—Fiction.
Classification: LCC PR9408.M273 S433 2021 (print) | LCC PR9408.M273
  (ebook) | DDC 823.92—dc23
LC record available at https://lccn.loc.gov/2020043047
LC ebook record available at https://lccn.loc.gov/2020043048

1

I SWEAR on the belly button of my only sister, my precious sister who hangs from my family by a watermelon's stem, and on the Sixty Holy Chapters that the following account is as true as you are sitting there.

May I have my days shortened, die of the big C on a Thursday forenoon, pray toward the northwest, be buried with my face toward the west, lose my firstborn male, be dishonored in front of the imam and the king of Marrakesh, lose my sister and my mother on the same day, slip on discarded dirty water on the southwest corner of my tent, get my hair cut on a Wednesday, visit my dead on a Sunday, be hit by the tazabbout of Sheikh Serigne; may I forget the names of the five holy mountains, those mountains that every believer must know, the mountains unperishable until the end of time, the Sinai, Sham, Mecca, Medina, and Jerusalem. God forbid, may all that I would wish to befall my enemy befall me if I'm telling you anything but the actual true story of Ahmed and Zarga.

I know you've heard the story. Everybody has. As God has watered our veins in the garden of happiness and dried the veins of all bad people in the place of sorrow and loneliness, so have wise and righteous men through the years related to us the story of Ahmed and Zarga. But what I'm about to tell you is the only true version of the story, the real and complete thing, as my sister told it to me. She heard it from our neighbor, old Aunt Aicha. You know Aicha, who knows everything about our old ways, who knows all the stories of the Bedouins and of the great

Calife Harun al-Rashid and how he built his hanging garden at the shore of the sea at the end of the world. People say, and she doesn't deny, that she is a direct descendant of Shahrazad, the greatest storyteller of all time, who saved her life by telling true stories to her husband for a thousand and one nights. Old Aunt Aicha entrusted to my sister the true story of Ahmed with the bone of her tongue.

And as my sister told it to me, I will tell it exactly that way to you. I am speaking about the dead, those who have already witnessed the truth firsthand, and I do not dare to say anything but the bare truth. The dead could not tell lies, even if they wanted to; that is why everything we see in our dreams, if it comes from the mouth of a dead person, is a hundred percent true. Don't you see? This is why the beyond is called the house of truth: all you need to experience it is to close your eyes for the last time. And everybody knows the curse that befalls those who tell lies about the departed, because they can hear everything we say about them; how else can you explain their awesome power? Ahmed himself, who herded camels on this earth in the tribe of Idamoor and who lives now in the house of truth, would not look down on me and tell me, "You haven't spoken the truth, oh living in the house of lies."

I don't need to tell you about the tribe of Idamoor, whose ancestors can be traced all the way back to the man who brought the first camels from Sham. The tribe has been herding camels ever since. They know everything about camels: how to feed them and water them, how to medicate them and use them to help medicate themselves, and how to drive and track them. Do you think it is easy to herd camels? But it is said that the Idamoor can drive anything. Ahmed's grandfather, the story goes, once drove a mixed herd of his camels and the camels of his neighbor. The night was so dark he couldn't have seen his finger if he held it before his eyes. All night he drove the herd by feel, because the presence of all his camels put his heart and mind at peace.

The problem was the neighbor's camels, especially a particularly feisty one that kept drifting away from the herd. Ahmed's grandfather was the strongest and most agile man who ever lived, a man who could eat a whole goat in one sitting, and so he managed each time to get the strange camel back on track. He arrived at camp, exhausted, just before the break of dawn. At sunrise, the people of the freeg were amazed at the wild ostrich that Ahmed's grandfather had herded and tamed.

For Ahmed, love for the nobility of camels was in his blood. He'd learned the skills of herding from his father, as his father had from his grandfather, and so forth and so on. He lived and breathed herding and couldn't picture himself away from his herd; it was the reason he existed. It was just like goats and chickens, where the one can't live without the other. His father never taught him herding; he just lived it and felt it as he accompanied his father, starting as far back as he could remember. Through his father, he first absorbed the names and attitudes of the individual camels. He loved the names, which are the most important things, because without names we cannot communicate or refer to the simplest of things. Like his father, he learned to tame the camels with love rather than violence; he used the thin stick he carried only for balance when he was riding, never as a weapon to abuse the camels. He could milk with one hand as the other hand held the adriss, the blessed wooden bucket he himself had made. He could brand, tail, and track with his eyes closed. He could predict where his herd would go on any particular day, in any weather. Like all true camel herders, he was smart, intuitive, lighthearted, and funny. Most important of all, he had a beautiful voice and sang the most beautiful hidas to guide and calm his camels.

In the old days, when the southern part of the country was a lush green carpet during the rainy season, Ahmed's great-grandfather had a huge herd that numbered several hundred head. This was even after he gave away one hundred pregnant she-camels as blood money to a poor family whose seven-year-old son was killed when he was trampled by another young mother in his herd. The boy naively tried to mess with her newborn baby; threatened, she lashed out, smashing his legs and tripping over his head. The local hajjab tried to save his life, but the child's head injury allowed the demons to suck the life out of his body, and he soon succumbed to his wounds.

That evening, the wise man was sitting under a big tree, watching his herd water. He was filling his pipe and brewing his tea when the heartbroken lady came to him. It is said he never changed his manner or put his pipe down. That evening, his mouth filled with the pipe, he merely gestured to his oldest son. The son immediately led the woman to the huge sea of camels that surrounded the water source, waiting for the branding of the younger members. The son told the woman to pick and choose. Despite the pain of losing her child, a pain that cut her heart that much worse because he had just earned the henna tattoo that commemorates the accomplishment of memorizing a quarter of the Holy Quran, she immediately stopped crying and wailing, perhaps in her shock over becoming rich in the time it takes to milk a tame she-camel. Money and camels do not necessarily make you happy, but they can put a sense of security in your heart, making it harder for the demons to put doubt in it.

Ahmed was not as rich as his great-grandfather, or his grandfather, or even his father, because the successive years of droughts had eaten away at the family's herd. Ahmed knew too well that the day would come when the camels would disappear, because old times were better than his times, and the times after him would be still worse. That sad and dark day would come when all of the family's camels were gone, and that day would be the end of time. He knew the end of time was very near: the signs manifested themselves everywhere. So many people dreamt about it, and the more they dreamt it, the more the ruthless drought was accelerating the process. People can only live when camels live, and the disappearing camels were a clear sign that humans would soon follow.

It is bad luck to speak about the exact number of your camels, because evil eyes are everywhere and they are hungry, and as the number of camels in the freeg has dwindled, the evil eyes have become that much more effective and evil. What we know for sure was that the previous Ramadan, Ahmed gave a three-year-old camel in zakat for the poor, which would put his herd somewhere between forty-six and sixty-one camels. He donated the camel discreetly, of course, steering clear of the taboo. The only time Ahmed discussed the number of his herd was when he paid taxes to the French, who would count the animals to the very last one. Dues to Allah and to his tribesman, dues to the French colonizer: like all Bedouins of his time, Ahmed found himself subject to two traditions and two systems; he accepted both as they presented themselves, as he knew to do in order to live and die a happy man. And the number of his camels, fortunately, never went beyond Ahmed, the governors, and the translator.

Animals, too, have their systems, and in the kingdom of camels a single bull rules, a patriarch that leads the whole herd. Nothing is tolerated within the herd but total loyalty and subjugation to this all-wise, all-knowing, all-powerful leader. With the group's interests at heart, the bull decides which direction his herd takes and what ground it will graze, watching over it to make sure none slip away and chasing away unwanted intruders, both camel and human. Though he answers to a human owner, every decent herder knows he can make no decision regarding his herd without the tacit understanding of the bull. This mutual respect and cooperation between bull and herder is the secret to the peace and harmony that has reigned over Bedouin life since the day the sweet singing of an Egyptian farmer caused the first camel to emerge from the Nile.

This relationship between bull and herder was nowhere closer than in the matter of the perpetuation of the breed. Like every decent man of his time, Ahmed trusted the wisdom of the head of his herd, which meant not just letting the bull lead the herd as he chose, but letting him mate when and how he saw fit. The bull, in turn, knew to trust the judgment of the herder when human-assisted husbandry was necessary. As a boy, Ahmed had watched a thousand times as his father and other herders helped bulls mount young she-camels in the field of the well, the whole camp gathered around him to witness the beauty of the conception of a camel. Ahmed learned the herders' moves this way, as he learned so many skills, and when the time came he performed them so automatically that he couldn't understand how anyone else would find them difficult or unnatural.

Husbandry of this kind served a particular purpose: to increase the chances of a female offspring. Ahmed, like his father and his father's father, knew it was a sin to pretend he could determine the sex of a new addition to the herd; all decent herders understand they are merely instruments who can provide the right conditions for a baby she-camel to be produced. They know which she-camels are likely to produce female offspring. They know that the time of the year, the month, the day, what direction the she-camel faces during copulation, even how the bull penetrates, all play a role in determining the sex of the baby camel.

And as with breeding, so with the prevention of breeding. There can be only one uncastrated bull in the herd. Two bulls will fight to the end; one will end up exiled or dead, dishonored and unsung. If one of them is killed, people will not even eat the meat, because it stinks and tastes bad. And so just as he learned by watching as a child how to assist in the propagation of the herd, so Ahmed learned to castrate the male offspring, not for the happiness of the bull, because there can be no happy life for one who must court many females at the same time, but for the safety and the good of the herd. Not knowing any better, he started by practicing on the small pets his father brought him; he castrated his small cat, just as he'd seen his father castrating the camels. The cat suffered, but all the kids who were gathered around were laughing, having sinful fun. At first Ahmed felt the cat's pain, but when he looked around and everyone was laughing, he started laughing nervously, too, and enjoying the scene. And the others joined in the work, handing Ahmed the hot rod to burn the wound and make it heal faster.

Afterward his grandmother was angry with him. She scolded him and explained to him that "Allah tortures those who torture animals and people." He saw immediately that this was true: the image of the cat's suffering rushed in and haunted him, as it haunted his friends, until they made amends and promised not to do it again.

If only Ahmed's cousin had learned that lesson! Everyone knows the story: Ahmed's cousin, who grew up with Ahmed and who should have known better, one day grew so angry with his bull that he beat the animal before the herd, dishonoring and humiliating him in front of the she-camels who trusted and admired him and lived under his protection. The she-camels lost all sense of security in that moment, seeing that a skinny Bedouin would dare to abuse their huge and powerful protector.

It was a reprehensible act, his cousin knew, and he immediately regretted the rage that Satan had whispered into his head. He knew the sin of abuse made him eligible for both the punishment of God and the retaliation of the bull. And he knew too well that if God is all-forgiving, there is no such forgiveness from a dishonored bull. Sure that retaliation was imminent, Ahmed's cousin decided to get rid of the bull by selling it to another tribe, compounding the bull's pain by sending it into exile.

Ten years passed, but a bull never forgets. One day, on one of his journeys, the cousin invited himself into a Bedouin camp to take a lunch break and a nap before resuming his trip. The camp, of course, turned out to belong to the same tribe to whom he'd sold the bull. When he caught sight of the old animal he froze in terror; the fear lay in his legs, as they say in the desert. The inner weakness he had manifested in his violence against the animal was obvious now to everyone, including the bull. And yet the bull made no move toward him, leading the foolish man to believe he had forgotten the beating. Feeling safe and tired, and swayed by a host who swore by Allah he would divorce his wife three times if he refused the hospitality, the cousin decided to spend the night in the camp.

In the dead of the night, when the cousin was sound asleep, the bull followed the smell of his nemesis and snuck into the tent. He could have crushed the sleeping man, but out of respect for the host he didn't make a mess. Instead he wrapped his front legs around his tormentor's head and squeezed him to death. No one else was harmed; no one even woke. In the morning they found the guest resting in peace, looking normal in every way but with a head the size of a small Turkish meatball.

Ahmed no more judged the bull for this than he would question and condemn the chief of his clan. As there is only one bull in the herd to lead and protect, so there is just one elder who leads and protects the freeg; like the bull, the chief is caring but harsh, decisive, and uncompromising. Life in the vast ocean of desert is brutal and unsparing: resources are scarce, water is precious, and grazing ground is the great zero-sum game. A Bedouin spends his entire life in survival mode, the stakes are high for every decision, and hesitation can easily be fatal. And so the motto is One Chieftain, One Leader, One Single Option to be followed.

Like many in his clan, Ahmed did not love his tribal leader, for he could be heartless and vengeful and brutal, but he respected him, and tried never to disturb the peace of his clan. He was a practical man, and given the choice of facing the desert alone, hungry and exposed, or sticking with the group and seeking its protection and warmth, he happily chose the latter. Ahmed had spent days on end without food. He had been beaten and abused by strangers, and suffered even more horrible things that he would never speak of, ever. He knew the key to being a success-ful camel herder is total cooperation with the bull, and living in complete harmony with the herd, as a member of its family. The way to be one with the herd was through fusion and surrender.

2

THIS YEAR was especially dry; one could hardly speak of rain at all. To Ahmed, it was a clear sign that the day of judgment was coming, when all the animals would die and only humans would be left to fight and kill themselves. The few people he knew who had made the Hajj had witnessed dark signs and heard chilling stories, and had returned to the freeg full of tales of the approaching end of time.

As the summer of the long dry year came to a close, everybody was waiting on the rain, most of all the camels. Like his herd, Ahmed was nervous, and he knew he needed to keep a close eye on them. But he was not overly worried. The imam had already called the al-Istiska, the traditional prayer in which the imam and the people turn their oldest outer garments inside out as a sign of humility and poverty and raise their hands toward the sky in supplication. And for the past week sandstorms had swept the region, as they do just before the rains begin.

Ahmed's days began early. With the first azan, before the last call of "Prayer is better than sleep," he would crawl from beneath the skin blanket that protected him from the biting cold of the desert. He would take a drag or two on his pipe to straighten up his head, and check Jamila, his wife, and his son, Abdallahi, to make sure they were well. Then he would step out of his tent to feel the energy of the presence of his herd, which had been stirred to impatience by the sound of the imam reciting al-Fatiha in his sweet, hoarse voice. The herd acted on cues, and the Subuh prayer, carried so clearly on the quiet morning breeze, before the freeg was fully awake and chattering, was its cue. To keep the herd from wandering at night, Ahmed tied the forelegs of a few older she-camels, knowing the bull would never leave the matriarchs and lead the herd away. At the imam's voice, the camels knew the she-camels would soon be untied and they all would be freed from their restrictions.

Ahmed paused a moment and breathed deeply, drawing himself up to his full height. He was just tall enough to pet the tip of the hump of his tallest camel without stretching. In his day he had taken down many bigger men in the freeg's wrestling competitions, and he could still lift the biggest full water bucket and empty it in the pool. His grandmother once told him he was born in the year of the Fall of the Stars, but no one could say how many years ago that had been. Ahmed knew that he was on the downhill part of his earthly journey, and he also knew that there was nothing bad or good about age. He lived his life's stages instinctively and effortlessly, like everyone else in the freeg. Subscribing to Allah's will and the plan that Allah laid out for him, knowing that both bad things and good things pass, he faced the dawn as he did every morning: content.

Ahmed finished his prayers quickly and called for Abdallahi: camels give milk only if they want to, and milking must be done before the she-camels are fully awake and shrink their udders, purposely refusing to release milk even for their babies. Ahmed took a piece of dry wood and started rubbing a thin stick against it until it sparked and began to burn. Abdallahi helped his father warm up the adriss, letting the flames touch it just until it smoked and released the sweet smell of old burnt milk. Ahmed had a gift for carving. He had crafted not only the necessary objects of Bedouin life but also beautiful animals, like the camels he gave Abdallahi as toys. But the adriss was his prize. Using a small ax, he had sculpted its rough shape out of the trunk of the adriss tree, scooping it out slowly and leaving only a thin layer. He'd carved two grips along the top edge that held the rope and laid in the metal rings that strengthened the bucket and gave it its robust beauty. He'd rubbed in the special grease from cow's fat to season it and protect it from worms, and let it sit for many days. Then, using fire and dry paint, he'd made the simple drawings that were his signature. Even now it was still being completed: before each milking, he would expose the inside of the bucket to fire until it started to smoke, and so every day the milk it collected tasted better.

Ahmed always started with the easiest camels to milk, since camels like to mimic each other, and the rest would follow suit. Sawda, who was one of the oldest, was an easy task; she stood up as soon as she saw the man and boy approaching. Ahmed gently removed the cover from her udder and gave her a couple of tugs and let her baby suckle until her teats swelled. Then Ahmed brushed the baby aside and milked until the boy could hardly hold the adriss anymore, only then letting the baby back in. The boy sat beside the fire and drank from the warm milk, leaving a thick layer of foam around the tip of his nose and mouth, then emptied the rest into the big wooden bowl that his mother had prepared, leaving only a small splash in the adriss for good luck for the next milking.

Then, as the boy watched, Ahmed fed his camels as his father had, and as his father had learned from his grandfather; each generation knew that you could never go wrong by following the ways of your forefathers. Camels grazed grass and branches on their own, but they needed herders to cut their fur and bring them the snow-white salt that was a crucial part of their diet. Ahmed set the bowl of salt before them, reminding them to appreciate the sweet grass, too, and remember the camels in China who were forced to eat only salt throughout the year. Finally, pulling out an aspirin bottle filled with motor oil that his cousin had brought from Dakar, he medicated his camels. He dipped the tip of his index finger into the Water of Hell, as it was known in the area, and applied it around the udders of the she-camels, where the ticks loved most to bury their heads under the skin, and around the armpits and inner thighs of the rest of the herd. Finally, with the herd medicated, petted, and satisfied, Ahmed untied the forelegs of the elder she-camels, freeing them to lead the herd away. Camels bear no resentments about the past and no hopes for the future, and if the moment calls for happiness and optimism, they are happy and optimistic. Calling "Hey!" he lightly but firmly tapped Sawda on her upper thigh, and throughout the herd ears rose and twitched at the announcement of a new and exciting day.

Returning to Abdallahi, Ahmed removed a glowing piece of charcoal from the fire and put it in a small tea furnace. He heated the water until it boiled and drank the first round, which was too strong for the child's stomach, while the little boy warmed his hands and feet and waited to be given a sip or two of tea from the second pouring. The morning chill wasn't fooling anyone—the dry north wind promised a hot day—but the boy stayed as close as he could to the fire. They shared Jamila's morning menu, the dry cookies and Sudanese nuts she always prepared for them in the morning. The sun started to climb, pushing the child away from the dying fire, and Ahmed slurped the last sip out of the last cup of tea, wishing, like always, for just a little more.

"Empty the guirbahs!" Ahmed called to a group of children that had gathered near his tent. It was his day to water the freeg, and the children had brought their parents' goatskins and their donkeys. Fetching water was the children's job, but they needed a grown-up to draw the water and pour it into the pool so they could fill the guirbahs. In truth, this used to be the job of slaves, but that ended when Ahmed's father had a terrible dream. In his dream he died, and in death the trader who sold the family slaves came and enslaved him. The trader put a thick cold chain around his neck and beat him with a thick stick to drive him toward a burning pit. Ahmed's father tried to shout, but because he had already died, he had no voice. Inches from the pit, one of his own slaves struck the chain, cutting it with his bare hands and freeing his master, and sending the slave trader into the pit. Ahmed's father awoke terrified and sweating, so changed that he not only set his own slaves free but swore on the Quran, while facing Mecca, to buy the slaves of others and set them free as well until the day he died.

It took half a day to make the round trip for water, and by the time Ahmed and the children returned, two full guirbahs strapped together on each side of every donkey, the shade was starting to pull slowly to the east. He ate, drank tea, and took a nap, waiting for the day to cool off so he could go and gather his camels.

The camels had been wandering on their own all day, but Ahmed knew his herd better than he knew the fingers of his hands, and he felt them as he would feel his human family. He trusted them enough to give them total freedom, knowing that full contact with his herd would be burdensome to him and his camels. Camels are not goats, and they most certainly are not cows; they are somewhere in between. Goats need the constant attention and physical presence of the herd. Cows can be controlled by their babies; if you keep the babies close, the cows will go off and graze and come back using the exact same path. Camels need both freedom and company. They enjoy their time with the herder, but constant company is the negation of their freedom. They get sick and die of depression when the herder fails to understand that they need time alone, when they can discuss in their own language the things they cannot discuss in front of humans.

Although he did not speak their language, Ahmed generally knew what was in the minds of his camels. He knew how they thought and where they would go on a particular day. He knew the effect of the seasons and the weather conditions on the camels, and he almost always knew where to go to get back his herd. In the rainy season, when the camels were happiest, they would stay close. But this time of year, when grazing grew scarce and the herd wandered nervously throughout the day, even a seasoned herder like Ahmed would struggle to keep up with their ever-changing plans and moods. They could cover up to thirty kilometers on the driest, windiest days, and sometimes he would not reach them until the sun started to drop toward the west after Asr prayer.

Once, a few years before, Ahmed met a Frenchman who said his job was to write about people and publish the stories so other people could read them—or spread gossip, as the people of the freeg say. The Frenchman asked Ahmed how he knew which way to go when he went off to gather his herd. It was hard for Ahmed to answer.

"There's not much to it," he had said. "If you're missing someone you love, you go looking for them in the places they love most." Camels are no different, he explained. They always returned to the same places where they once found happiness, good company, and fresh grass.

In fact, bringing back his herd was routine for Ahmed. He would fasten his boubou around his waist and start in the direction his instincts led him. When he saw the first footprints, he would determine the general direction they were heading, put the tracks to one side, and follow a straight line. If he felt he was getting too far away, he would drift slowly toward the prints. It was like a game of chess, predicting what your opponent's next move would be. Every time he crossed the prints, he'd leave them to a side and make a mental note. When enough time passed without crossing the prints, he adjusted toward the side he'd memorized last. He could always smell his herd before seeing it. Nothing made him happier than seeing his herd, fully assembled together, safe and sound, playing and fully grazed.

But no matter which direction he chose, he always started out from his tent due southwest, as tradition demands, for it is a good omen to do so, following in the footsteps of our Prophet.

And so he set off that afternoon, absentmindedly mumbling the usual prayer:

> We're going out as Mohamed—peace be upon him—did,
> from Mecca to Medina.

Before long, a sand hill on his right blocked his way. He changed course slowly, drifting to the left and aiming toward the south, then shifting ever so slightly to the east. The camels undoubtedly would have followed the faint whiff of a cooler breeze from the south in search of grass, or even rain after the long dry season. Ahmed thought he could smell the breeze trying to force itself through the waves of heat and the powerful seasonal hot north wind that was eating up every green tree, leaving a wildfire-like trail of devastation on the ground and desperation in the hearts it left behind. But he couldn't say for sure if he was smelling the sweet wind, or if it was his memory and desire that was smelling it. Either way he had to follow it, because when he started out that morning he linked his soul with the souls of his herd, and real or not, what he smelled and felt at that moment was what they, too, were smelling and feeling.

He stopped for a moment by a bare tree. He was in a hurry now, eager to reach the herd while there was still light, and his pants were restraining his pace. Extra clothing like these baggy pants, the new burdens of civilization, had recently, needlessly been introduced into Bedouin life. A Bedouin learns early on that every unnecessary piece of clothing costs a third of his energy, and a gentleman who knows how to hold his boubou in place has no need of pants. But now even men like Ahmed had to wear pants to appear decent and whole, and young people had even begun to wear those shirts that stick to the skin and stink.

The hot, battering winds had exposed the tree's roots, scarred by the many years of drought and resistance when the rainfalls were few and far between. Ahmed's heart ached for the parched tree, and he wondered how much longer it could last without rain. He quickly undid his long, thin leather belt and let the pants drop to the ground. Then he slung them over his left shoulder, holding them in place with the stick he carried behind his neck. His pace doubled, and with his longer steps the breeze was growing stronger. He soon came across the first faint sets of footprints and fell into the rhythm of tracking, drifting slightly right or left, depending on the wind. He found himself singing a song he'd heard on the radio someone had recently brought from Dakar:

> Ask the sweet lady with the black veil:
> What have you done to the righteous and God-fearing man!
> He was just about to go to prayer; he put on his clothes and
>   headed to his mosque
> And you walked by and ruined his mood and concentration
> Give him back his prayer, and by our holy Prophet kill him not
> O God! O God!
> You turned me into a child!

Ahmed walked on, unaware of the distance he was putting behind him until thirst reminded him to take a sip or two from his guirbah. He took a very small one, so as not to shock his dry throat and empty stomach, and then a bigger one, and saved the biggest one for last. As the cold water settled, he could feel the presence of the herd.

When he climbed the hill just to his right he saw Mahmoud, the goatherder, hurrying to drive his charges home, fearing the hungry wolves that close in under the protection of the darkness. He felt a wave of gratitude that his forefathers were not goatherders, so he didn't have to follow their ways or live the rest of his life in shame by abandoning them. He couldn't imagine being glued to his herd from sunrise to sunset. People say that goatherders are possessed, and so they fall in love with herding the wrong animal.

Ahmed could just make out his own herd ahead, a little to the right of due south. A broad smile spreading across his face, he descended the small valley between two long dunes.

"Hey, hey!" he shouted, letting them know that they had company. They showed their recognition by not startling or changing what they were doing. He passed quickly through the scattered herd and climbed the dune on the right. He descended again and climbed the ridge to the left to get a better look. But he could only see what he couldn't see: not the herd, but what was missing. It always amazed him how people see more clearly the things they don't have than the things they do have, but now none of his camels were good enough to make him forget what he wasn't seeing.

Zarga was missing. Zarga, whose name means blue in Arabic and who was named that because she was a blue camel, which is a camel with dark fur and white patches. She was just two and a half years old. Ahmed scanned the field around the grazing herd, and ran again up a nearby hill to get a wider look. But Zarga was nowhere to be found. She'd become a white eye lost in the red wind, as the saying goes. At first he was in total disbelief, but slowly the cold truth hit him. He felt a current of sadness running up his head and down into his spine and limbs.

He didn't panic. Ahmed knew he was up against a fast-sinking sun, and in the darkness of the night, without the shining moon, there would be no chance for any quick find. He made a hurried last scan of the surrounding hills, then turned his attention to the herd. Camels know when one of their own leaves, and while they are very sad, they believe in the total freedom of every member to separate if it chooses. As long as they are inside the herd, they have to abide by the herd's rule, but they would never force another member to do what it doesn't want to do.

As the sun set, Ahmed absentmindedly watched the camels take their last bites, hissing as their snouts fought through the thorny branches into fat, fresh leaves. He mumbled the late-afternoon supplications he'd learned from listening to his father repeat them over and over every day around the same time, just before the sun hit the Ocean of the Oceans.

I take refuge in Allah, using his words from everything He created,
And there is no power but from Allah
Allah the Highest, Allah the Greatest.

He'd learned many short Surats just by hearing his father recite them. And before that, before he was able to memorize, he would mimic his mother's prayers, making all the moves she made and moving his lips when his mother spoke a supplication. The things that Ahmed had learned this way stuck with him better than those he'd deliberately studied.

When the sun was down, Ahmed did his Maghrib prayer quickly—very quickly. He wasn't able to concentrate, thinking of all the terrible things that might be happening to Zarga. He did no ritual washing before doing his prayers, a luxury he couldn't afford: water cannot be wasted in the desert. Only the camp's imam washed before prayer. Ahmed took a shower only occasionally, pouring water from the pool over his body after a long day of drawing water for his herd and the camp. He never used soap like women do, because he didn't want his skin to be smooth or light. That would make him vulnerable to the sun, to thorns, or to his camels. He needed a thick skin.

He touched the clean, grainy sand. It had been baking all day long, but had cooled enough now to give a good warm caress to Ahmed's tired skin. He smoothly wiped his hands, tapped the ground with both palms, and wiped his face, making sure he touched everywhere, horizontally between his two ears, and vertically between his hairline and his chin. He slapped the ground one more time with his palms and wiped his arms with the clean sand. Ahmed had performed Tayammum a million times. He had learned the steps from the mouth of his imam as he had repeated them on countless occasions, telling Ahmed that he didn't need to wash when water was scarce or he was far away from a water source. His imam had told him that sand was pure, and purifying, too.

Ahmed led the herd, fighting his way through the darkness that enveloped him and erased the beautiful desert landscape.

The darkest part of a night is the beginning, because the eyes need time to adjust to the dark and small demons try to cover the stars to scare humans and animals. In time, though, the stars discover the trick and shine through, as does the moon when he isn't on vacation. The night had intruded without asking permission, though he wished it had asked: he could have used some daylight to look for the straying Zarga.

In daylight, tracking a stray would be easy. He would trace the herds' prints back until one set split off, and work from there. If the wind had wiped the prints away, he would go by instinct, pretending to be the lost one and letting his body follow the easiest way, the way that made him happiest, avoiding the spots where demons live, like old firepits and places where blood has been spilled. But that would have to wait. For now, as he led the cooperative herd back to the camp, he was left only with his imagination.

What could have happened to Zarga? She might have been stolen. It happened all the time: raiding tribal gangs from the far north would come and drive herds back home, leaving nothing but dust, frustration, and despair behind. But a raiding gang would have driven the whole herd away, and even if he had been standing guard, he couldn't have stopped them. Those gangs were heavily armed and ready to fight, and Ahmed refused to carry a gun. His mother had taught him that guns are tools the devil can use against innocent people, and one should never carry them around because the devil himself could take over and load the weapon and pull the trigger, killing someone against the will of the owner. How many men had been victimized like that? Far too many to count. Ahmed had heard plenty of sad stories about innocent victims. True, he had never seen a demon use a gun, but his decency and honesty wouldn't allow him to question established facts as they were handed down from generation to generation. And he understood the lesson. The problem with killing, his mother would say, was that you can always repent the sin, make amends, even give reparation to those you've harmed, but nothing you can do will bring the dead back to life.

There was another possibility. Animals are social beings (they are just like Bedouins, except they speak a different language), and as long as they're healthy and well oriented they will stick with the family. But in a big melee of herds, when two herds meet, an animal can lose its way and go with the wrong family. Ahmed had heard earlier that day that some herding families coming from the south were heading north. Zarga might have strayed and joined them, without anyone noticing. Sometimes the stray animal comes back on its own, or the strange herder, if he is honest, forces it to split off and go back to its herd. Or Zarga might have strayed into one of the herds of a neighboring camp, or even another herd from his own camp.

But with the many terrible things that could be taking place, Ahmed couldn't afford such wishful thinking. And how would he break the news to Abdallahi? The boy had been begging to ride Zarga since she was a baby: grownups rode adult camels, Abdallahi reasoned, so logically children should be able to ride small camels. It was a plausible idea, but for the fact that camels aren't born with the idea that humans will ride them, and so must go through the hard process of learning to follow a human's instructions. Zarga was just now reaching the age when she could be tamed, and the boy's begging only increased by the day. How could Ahmed tell him now that she was missing?

And in truth, Zarga represented more to Ahmed than a companion for Abdallahi and promising breeding cow. During the great drought that had swept the country years ago, Ahmed's grandfather fell very ill. Neither the traditional doctors, the hajjabas, nor the French doctors could help him. Even the great Dr. Kaufmann gave up on him. Ahmed had watched with his own eyes as that strong man, a man who had made a difference in so many people's lives, withered away, dying slowly in great pain and suffering. A man with a long life of dignity, courage, honor, and caring for others couldn't even take care of his own business. The stench of his urine filled the air around his tent.

On the day he died, Zarga's grandmother refused to leave the pen. When the herds left for grazing, she remained in the camp, circling the tents and crying loudly in a heartbreaking voice. When the revered man was taken to his grave, the animal followed the procession solemnly. When he was buried and the people returned to the camp, the camel wouldn't leave the grave-yard. She kneeled between him and the kiblah for days, refusing food or water until she died. The family allowed her to rest in peace beside the man.

The family took the camel's actions to be a clear sign of his grandfather's reverence, purity, and closeness to Allah. For Ahmed, who was respected everywhere he went because of his father and who bore the legacy of his grandfather, bringing Zarga home meant more than restoring a camel to his herd.

From far off, Ahmed could see the silhouettes of the tents in the freeg and hear the cacophony of the babies' cries, the goats' bleats, the camels' grunts, and the shouts of women calling their playing children home so they could blow evening supplications on their heads before it got too dark. The smell of the mrah, where the camels spend the night, grew more intense with every step toward the freeg. But neither the sound nor the smell was as usual.

3

THE PLAN was simple. He would milk the camels as soon as the
dust settled, when the animals quieted and settled down and the
moon brightened. He was tired, but he couldn't afford to be. His
belt still around his boubou—though with the day's sweat holding it in place he hardly needed a belt—he filled his bone pipe and
went to ask around the neighborhood.

> Peace be with you!
> Peace be with you!
> What's new?
> Hopefully good news!
> No bad news!
> Hopefully no one is sick!
> Hopefully good news!
> Hopefully no one's suffering!
> How are the animals?
> How's grazing?
> Did you cross any paths?
> No. Hope no evil happened!
> Hope all's well! Anyone sick?
> MashaAllah? So, what's new?

Bedouin greetings, small talk of a sort: each talking over the
other, repeating the exact same thing and always giving good and
positive answers, even if the news was not good. The only part of
the conversation that was of interest to Ahmed was the question
about the paths, but he came up dry. No one had seen Zarga.

Ahmed had a trustworthy friend, five-year-young Laamesh,
who would carry him on his journey. The name means Squinter;

Laamesh was called that for the way he squinted in the presence of company he didn't trust. He was, for Ahmed, a faithful ride indeed.

Laamesh was castrated, which made him skinnier, quicker, and easier to ride. It also made him smell much better and act friendlier with others. Laamesh was the nice kid in the family; he gave more than he took. His mother, Mabrouka, had died a year ago, after a very long and fruitful life that included bearing three females in a row, and Ahmed hadn't forgotten Laamesh's pain when his mother died. He did not eat for three days, and cried for a full week.

Ahmed and Laamesh shared many good memories, and bad ones as well. They knew and respected each other. He never needed to chase Laamesh or compel him to do anything he didn't want to. To put the tether in Laamesh's snout piercing, he just gestured and the camel came.

Ahmed was sad and anxious, but also excited about the good company Laamesh would make in the treacherous, endless desert. He'd sing him the best hidas, songs sung for camels during long trips. Hidas are not only for the camels, but also for the herder himself. They take him to places no other person or thing can. Ahmed would sing from the wealth of hidas he'd memorized from listening to his father, and from those he had made up himself, many of them just by singing random words.

Laamesh was well fed and hydrated. He'd been to the well two days earlier, and could hold out five more days easily, in the harshest climate and without complaining. They could set out without delay.

Ahmed wasn't afraid to travel at night. He liked it. During the summer days, nobody could travel in the desert's scorching heat anyway. As his forefathers' wisdom said, *In the morning, the group is thankful that it traveled at night.*

Ahmed rested, waiting patiently as the thick darkness was washed away by the ever-brightening moon and shining stars. It was around the middle of the lunar month; there would be a full moon if the dust clouds allowed it, the auspicious time when the moon is so bright you can read the Arabic word "fatilan" on the moon's bright surface and Bedouins can find their fortunes inscribed there. But Ahmed had already determined that he would not look. A fortune can always change as long as one doesn't seal one's fate by reading it, and he was too afraid to face anything but good news. Besides, why even go on a trip if one already knows its end?

Instead he remained in the tent, in the company of Jamila and Abdallahi and the few belongings that served as furnishings: the straw mat, the two pillows, a big leather blanket, and the arahhal, the saddle Jamila used as a table when they weren't on the move. Jamila was grinding the corn she would spread over the cooked rice, sprinkling the kernels with water and striking them just hard enough to separate their outer shells. Ahmed glanced her way from time to time, following her progress absentmindedly.

Jamila was beautiful, and it only added to her beauty that she did not see herself that way. She was, according to many, Ahmed's ideal: at four fingers shorter than Ahmed, she was the perfect height, and at one and a half times her husband's weight, the perfect weight. She walked gracefully, swaying from one side to the other, taking care to move slowly, holding her eyes straight. In mixed company and among elders she spoke little, mostly listening, but she had memorized many poems that she sang with great skill and feeling, songs she sang through the days when the women of the freeg stitched the decorations on the woolen walls and ceiling of the newlyweds' tent, so that now the patterns themselves seemed to sing.

Jamila was talking to her husband now, not singing, but it was only the music of her voice that he heard. Distracted and drowning in his own thoughts, Ahmed sat with the adriss in his lap. The sweet smell of old milk coating the bucket from the morning carried him back to when he was a little child holding the bucket beneath the she-camel's udder while his father milked. He could barely reach high enough, and his hands would start to shake as the bucket filled. His father knew just when to give him a hand. He remembered the tickling mouths of the baby camels, their snouts running over his head and ears, around his neck, down his shoulders as they tried to force their heads between the boy and their mother's teats. He wouldn't even have measured up to the leg of a baby camel back then, but he knew they would never hurt him.

Ahmed nodded mechanically every once in a while in Jamila's direction, to give the impression he was listening. He was terrified of the moment his wife might ask for a response, but she hardly ever did; she mostly taught, and he gladly received. Common wisdom had taught Ahmed that people weren't interested in what he had to say as much as they were in expressing their own beliefs and opinions and offering all kinds of unsolicited advice. People love what they believe and only listen to what they themselves have to say. Though he tried to do better, he knew he was often the same way, so he was never shocked when he would tell people things and later on they would say they hadn't heard him. Inner ears are much stronger than outer ears.

The cries of the camp's children had slowly faded, like the ending of an Arabic song, as they were fed warm camel's milk and fell to sleep. He could hear the breathing of his sleeping wife now, who'd trailed off in the middle of a sentence. She'd been telling him about Abdallahi completing his fifth Hizb of the Quran; with fifty pages under his belt, the boy was through one-twelfth of the holy book. Ahmed was older before he had memorized that far; at his boy's age, he could recite only a decent-sized Surat or two. He was proud: he wanted so badly for Abdallahi to do all the things in life that he himself couldn't do, or wished he had done better. This did not mean he wished another life for his son. Like Ahmed, Abdallahi would not go to the French school; the elders of the freeg had so decided. He would memorize the Quran, master the basic books of Arabic grammar, and study Ibn Asher's primer on Malikite jurisprudence, and he would learn everything he needed to live and die a decent man. But Ahmed was impatient; he wanted his son to possess the wisdom of a forty-year-old, the age of maturity, when wisdom surpasses strength. He believed that if Abdallahi could both listen to his father and avoid his mistakes he could be the wisest Bedouin in the freeg.

Ahmed rose quietly and exited the tent. He could hear the steady, soft, musical regurgitation of his half-sleeping camels. He took a deep breath, inhaling the sweet, curing scent of the mrah, and quickly tethered Laamesh and set up the saddle. No one in the herd was startled, because Ahmed was one of them. But their apparent carelessness did not fool Ahmed; they were well aware that Zarga was missing, and they would not find it strange if he sought out one of them at this time. What would happen next the herd couldn't know, but the camels understood that something had to be done to bring back the missing one.

That word, "missing"! Every time Ahmed whispered it to himself, the devil forced another catastrophic scenario into his head. Zarga had been stolen and killed for meat by bandits from far, far away. God forbid! Someone was dining on her that very moment! Or demons themselves had taken her, as they had taken other camels that had simply vanished one day without a trace. Or worse, they had just taken her mind and her instincts, dooming her to wander until she died in the desert, alone. Ahmed shook himself, trying to break free from these horrible imaginings. If anything bad happened, it would break Abdallahi's heart. The camel was his, after all; what bad luck if he should lose his first camel ever, especially in a way as tragic as those the devil had been insinuating and whispering.

Looking at the endless sky, he wished there was a way for him to ascend high enough to see where Zarga was, high enough to see her fate. He wished he could write her name beside the stars for all the Bedouins to see, so they could point him to where

she was. But he knew that even if the sky looked close, it was
very far away. He knew, as a matter of fact, that a strong camel
running at a continuous gallop would take three hundred thirty-
three years, three months, three weeks, three days, and three
hours to reach the sky, or an Arabian horse five hundred years,
because while horses are quicker over short distances, camels will
overtake them because they can eat and run at the same time.

An idea came to him, one that made him consider for a moment returning to the tent to consult with Jamila. He had heard
the elders say that women can feel pain from far away. If a woman's child was hurt, she'd feel the pain in her stomach and her
ribcage around her breast. If Zarga was being hurt, Jamila would
have felt the pain and wouldn't have been able to rest. Then he
realized that Jamila, sleeping soundly, had already answered his
question.

4

AHMED MADE no sound. He wanted to leave as furtively as possible, and hoped he would be back home with Zarga by morning, before Abdallahi would even know that she'd been gone. His plan was to head south and go past where his herd had been earlier that day. As always, though, he started toward the southwest, the tradition he had learned from his father, who first recounted to him the story of our Prophet's migration from Mecca to Medina. In his mind he sang the prayer as his father would sing it aloud, in the sweetest of voices:

> We're going out as Mohamed, peace be upon him, did, from Mecca to Medina.

It was, Ahmed always thought, the perfect prayer; it wouldn't have mattered if his father knew no other prayers, because he could listen to this same verse over and over. But because extra precautions must be taken when setting out on a treacherous journey like this one, he added another.

> Noah, peace be upon him
> Noah, peace be upon him

Ahmed kept repeating this as he guided Laamesh outside the camp. His seasoned ride sensed his hurry, and seemed to struggle at first to keep up. As they left the camp behind, Ahmed added one more prayer, hoping to muzzle any demons that might cross his path.

Abdullah ibn Omar
Abdullah ibn Omar

This was another name he had learned from his father. Possession is a common practice of the evil spirits and even of the harmless jinn in the desert. The evil spirits possessed the Bedouins to harm them, and the good spirits mistakenly believed that by possessing them they could help them. This name would discourage both the demonic evil spirits and the meddling good ones from interfering with his plan. The bad spirits would burn as they approached the Bedouin, and the good ones would smell the protection from a thousand miles away and change direction. Ahmed repeated the name once more. He blew these supplications through the neck of his boubou onto his chest and again over Laamesh's head to give him the same protection. The rest he blew onto his palm and lightly rubbed on the top of his head, making sure his fingers touched the top of the skull through the thick and dirty hair.

For additional protection, both Ahmed and Laamesh were equipped with the hajabs that they wore around their necks, tiny charms wrapped in paper and covered and sealed with leather. Tampering with these charms by opening them and trying to see what was inside could cause permanent blindness or loss of the faculty of speech. His mother had bought him his charm when he was just a little boy, acquiring it from a street fruit vendor who worked as a hajjab and a traditional doctor on the side. When Ahmed saw a similar one for sale years later on his travels with his herd, he bought it to protect his favored ride.

The cool and eerily quiet night drew Ahmed on as he pulled Laamesh behind him. Nature's magnificence manifested itself in a clear sky and an infinite ocean of sand dunes in every direction. Everything everywhere looked exactly the same. The shining moon and the bright stars reflecting off the clean white dunes turned the night into day, and inexperienced travelers who didn't know how to read the stars would be easily disoriented.

It was so bright that after a time even Ahmed forgot it was night. He must have walked far, because he couldn't feel his feet anymore. But tired as he was, he didn't want to take advantage of Laamesh and ride him, at least not yet. He never rode for fun, vanity, or just joy; that would be a betrayal of the friendship and family connection that linked him to his camels. When he did mount Laamesh, he would tap him with the back of his heel, telling him silently to hurry up a bit, but not to run, because urging a camel to run is also a form of vanity. And though he had never been without a stick, he had never used it on his camels, not once. Using violence against camels would be an unspeakable and disgusting act, and most certainly an evil way to treat Laamesh after all that they had been through together. Ahmed's grandmother had told him that on the day of judgment Allah would avenge all of one's wrongdoings, especially those perpetrated against helpless animals.

Way into the dead of the night, he found himself riding in the comfortable saddle he had made from the finest wood and highest-quality leather. He caught himself drooling, and recognized that he was now in that state between wakefulness and sleep, when half of him was aware of where he was and the other half dreaming. He didn't know when he had mounted, or how long he had been riding. After confirming his direction, he drifted off again. The saddle was not a bad place to rest on long trips, as long as the devil didn't try to interfere with his camel and send him on the wrong path.

As he rode, an older lady from his camp appeared to him. It was Messouda, the one people turned to for help with their romantic relationships. Messouda was old—so old anyone who knew how old she was had died long ago—but alongside the camp's other elders, her small, energetic presence gave her an air of unusual health and youth. Now blood was gushing out of her small goat-like ears, though there was no sign she was suffering any pain. On the contrary, she was laughing wildly.

What did Messouda want with him? She was renowned for her proficiency in legzana, the art of reading randomly laid symbols to predict the future. She had supposedly learned it from a grigri master during a trip a long time ago to Dakar, Senegal. She was already an old woman then, and her strength and sharpness still had not weakened. She had always been bright. She had memorized many poems, new and old, as a child, she spoke Wolof, and if called upon she could predict, with almost surgical precision, the future romantic relationships between the young people of the camp. She generally used this power to bring people together, but she also served those who sought her advice in bringing down relationships, either out of jealousy or spite, or in order for a competing girl to win a desired boy, much to the detriment of his girlfriend.

Through the years she had claimed other powers as well, and once she even cheated to back up her claim. Like all Bedouin seers, she would read the stars and the clouds to predict the location and intensity of the rains, but she had heard from her cousin the French translator that the French could do so even better, thanks to their powerful telescopes, which allowed them to see the writing inside the clouds. Intrigued, she gave her cousin three goats to give to the French if they would share their prediction. He spoke to the weather officer, of course giving over just one of the goats and accomplishing the rest with flattery. When he returned, Messouda amazed her clients by predicting rain two days before it happened. When her trickery was revealed, she came crying to the imam and swore on the belly button of her only son that she would never make a deal with the devil again. She was soon forgiven, partly on the strength of her past record, partly because they had seen her suffer the loss of her husband and all of her children but one, and partly because she claimed to have seen and talked to the jinn. This they could neither prove nor disprove, much like the claim that she had a very powerful and rather vengeful tazabbout.

That tazabbout, that aura of vengeance, surrounded her now. Messouda bit at the air between her upper and lower teeth, in a sign she would bite him. She flew at him and seized his finger with her cold, damp hand; he felt as though it had been bitten off and was flying through the air. He jerked his hand back with such force he almost lost his balance and fell off of his saddle. He woke from his half-sleep, scratched his eyes, and mumbled some prayers to ward off the bad spirit.

> Allah: there is no god but He, the Ever-Living, the Self-Subsisting One by whom all things subsist. Slumber overtakes Him not, nor sleep. To Him belongs whatever is in the heavens and whatever is in the earth. Who is he that can intercede with Him but by His permission? He knows what is before them and what is behind them. And they encompass nothing of His knowledge except what He pleases. His knowledge extends over the heavens and the earth, and the preservation of them both tires Him not. And He is the Most High, the Great.

May God forgive old Messouda! Ahmed could maybe have imagined her taking the form of a black cat to toy with him, but he never thought she would go so far as to take such an ugly shape and torment him, when she should know better than anyone that a man this far from home was vulnerable to all kinds of preying spirits. Then again, this may have been forced on her, too. You can't get evil spirits to share privileged information or influence the behavior of others without them asking for something in return. When he was growing up he had an aunt who had no children. She had given birth to seven boys and girls, but all of them had died. She tried every hajjab and had even consulted a Senegalese grigri who charged her a big sum of money, two veils, one boubou, one cane of sugar, and two and half camels. She could afford everything except for the half of a camel, but the grigri insisted that the secret lay in that half. She consulted with her family, and they decided that a fat calf equaled half a camel. The grigri agreed, and promised that her child would survive.

The child survived, all right, but only for two years—just one year more than any of the other children. She protested, of course, but had to give up when the grigri master told her that she had failed to tell him that she had unwittingly angered a big demon family when she crossed a garbage dump northwest of her camp, just after sunset, and not far from the cemetery. Had she told him the truth, he wouldn't have touched the child, he said. And as for his salary, he wouldn't give it back because his demon friends had already claimed it. Her hands hit the dust, as the Bedouins say.

It gave Ahmed a chill in his spine whenever he thought about how much that poor lady had suffered and the unfair treatment she'd endured. She couldn't apologize to the demon family because back then there was no medium to interpret between them. Maybe she had other options; Sidi Mohamed, the French translator, hustler, and traveler, once overheard the French doctor claiming he could cure her without negotiating with any spirits, but it was too late for that. The moral of all of this, as far as Ahmed was concerned, was that no one, not even French doctors, should mess with demons, whatever kind of spiritual powers they might wield.

Shaken, Ahmed rode on, his heart pounding from what he'd seen, and from what he'd felt when Messouda touched him with her hands. Eyes can play tricks. Ahmed had seen fata morganas before. But the touch had been real.

5

THE BEST way to fight evil spirits is to deprive them of the kind of environment where they thrive. Sleepwalking or sleep-riding makes a man vulnerable to his enemy's attack, so Ahmed decided to call it a night. Looking at the constellations above him, he located the Pole Star and al-Doubb al-Kabir, the Big Bear. They indicated it was around three hours until morning prayer time, enough to give him a decent rest. Ahmed was looking for anything in this vast and wide desert that could be called a campsite. It is next to impossible to find a shelter in the middle of nowhere, and that was where he was.

He spotted a shrub, a titarek, standing majestically on the side of a smooth dune. Its long, bare roots had been exposed by the sustained wind, but it had not been felled. Ahmed had used these titarek for many things. Camels eat the smooth, leafless twigs, which both fatten them and increase their milk. Ahmed himself would eat the branches, flowers, and fruits. His family used the titarek to cure urine retention and smallpox, and ground the seeds and mixed them with oil to use as an eye lotion. They wove the twigs into strong mats. When Ahmed killed a goat, he cooked the meat on the green branches of the titarek. But most important of all, Ahmed once heard Messouda say that the demons don't like it.

Beside the small titarek Ahmed found a home for the night. He didn't remove the saddle because he didn't plan to stay longer than necessary. He tied Laamesh's forelegs together to make sure he would not go too far. The animal wanted to eat, since he hadn't had a chance during the long ride that day and needed a late-night meal to fuel up for the journey in the morning. Ahmed trusted Laamesh fully, but a lone camel can wander away and get lost quickly, lured by the scent of camel urine, which they can smell as far as a two days' ride away. Tying his camel's feet was not something Ahmed took lightly, but it was necessary. He wrapped the other end of the camel's tether around the top of the saddle, leaving it loose enough for the animal to move his neck freely and get to the hard-to-reach spots on the titarek.

Ahmed was asleep as soon as he hit the cool, clean sand. He did not resist, though sleeping now came with a cost. This was not the first time he had had to sleep without a roof, so he knew the sleep would be deep and sweet. But he also knew that if he survived the animals of the night he would wake up feeling as heavy as a dead cow. The desert dew permeates the body and makes it weak.

A sudden quick pinch on his left index finger pried him from his sleep. He had had no feeling of time. Was it a couple of minutes or many hours that he had been out?

He stood up in one quick move, still not fully awake or knowing where he was. He always needed adjustment time when he woke up, the two halves fighting, the sleeping side pushing him back down and the other pulling him to his feet.

The wakeful side of him soon had the upper hand. He rubbed his eyes to adjust them quickly to the fading moonlight and unfamiliar surroundings. He spotted a big desert viper, the chaser of camel riders, slithering away; the gripping fear didn't stop him from noticing the beautiful tracks she left behind her. Feeling the pinch on his finger, it didn't take him long to realize what a dire situation he was in. Tired as he was, the fact he had woken up was nothing short of a miracle. If he hadn't then, he wouldn't have ever. Never found, he would become a mournful story for generations to come.

He saw it clearly: like a neighbor of theirs whose only son had died of dehydration on the way to Timbuktu, his mother would lose her mind over him. She would never believe that he had died, no matter how many people swore on the Quran to that effect. That poor woman had gone from one freeg to the other claiming that one of the French translators sold him to the commander of the fort to send him to war overseas. Fearing she wouldn't survive the shock, her family hid his death from her as long as they could: at first they told her he was sick, then sicker, and then in a dire situation. When many months later they finally told her he had died, she called them liars and even co-conspirators with the French commander. She lived in pain, but with the hope that he would come back home one day when the war was over. She held on to that hope until the day she died, sad and defeated.

What a dire prospect, not to speak the Shahada before his death. Not to say goodbye to his family, not to forgive and ask forgiveness from them. Not to dictate his last will and testament. Not to be prayed over and buried properly by his imam in the cemetery of his family. What agony for his family, to imagine that the body of their father had been devoured by vultures, wild dogs, and cats, one piece at a time!

It took less than a second for all of these scenes to run through his head. It couldn't have been more, since the throbbing pain in his finger wouldn't allow him more. His finger was a living thing attached to his body, with a living and beating heart of its own. Ahmed knew that he had to act and act fast; it was simply a matter of life and death and nothing in between. If the poison spread to his brain and his heart, he could start to say his last prayer. Taking time to think was a luxury he couldn't afford. Going back home to find a hajjab who knew the trade of sucking out the poison invisibly by milking around the bite was not an option. Long before he reached the camp, he would be dead and gone, swallowed by the sand and buried by the wind.

He'd seen snakebites before. One time his young cousin was bit by a chaser of camel riders. Luckily, he wasn't far away from the camp, and he was immediately taken to the hajjab of the freeg. The hajjab recited a spell and told the family to kill a goat every day for thirty days and wrap the fresh stomach around the snake-bit leg, and to apply French creams and 3 percent antibiotic ointments, too. They did this, and every day the hajjab repeated the spell, and after the long and painful treatment he indeed survived, with a scar the size of a French coin.

Ahmed wished he could remember the hajjab's words, but the spells of all hajjabs are unintelligible. Those who used spells derived from the Islamic tradition spoke them so quickly the listener couldn't discern the words. Others had learned their spells from native tribes said to use black magic, and mumbled them in a language no one else could understand. Ahmed was no fan of black magic, which can backfire in ways that he didn't dare imagine, but he might have been ready to make an exception now, taking his chances on being turned into a black cat or monkey or much, much worse. But debating whether he would or wouldn't have risked it was pointless: good magic or black magic, with no hajjabs around he wasn't getting either.

There was one phrase he remembered: *Je suis malade.* His cousin Sidi Mohamed, the translator, taught him this magic sentence when he was a child, and it had stuck in his head ever since. But he had never used it, and did his best not to learn more French. He felt guilty and queasy inside every time he thought about the sin of speaking a foreign language, French in particular. Ahmed's grandmother had warned him that speaking a single French word could result in his prayers being denied for forty long days. Imagine what might happen to those who attended the free French school! The elders and imams had issued a verdict that going to French school was a clear violation of tribal ethics and religious values. Knowledge should be sought for its own sake and for the sake of Allah, they argued, rather than to acquire money, personal privilege, and social status, which was the case with the modern school. French schools groomed children to be self-righteous and arrogant and to look down on uneducated people. To go to them was to risk eternal damnation.

And yet Sidi Mohamed had once claimed that the French doctor could cure a snakebite with just one painful injection. But even if Sidi Mohamed was right, which he wasn't all the time, Dr. Kaufmann was even farther away, in Rosso, and Ahmed did not like to ride in cars. They disoriented him and made him nauseous, and he instantly lost all sense of distance and direction. He once vomited on the dashboard when he saw the trees and camels running in the opposite direction of the car. His mind could understand the concept, but making a three-day ride in a couple of hours made no sense to his body. And even so, to get to the doctor would take at least a week. He would first have to get to the dirt road, and then try his luck with passing cars. He would never make it.

He knew what had to be done. To prepare himself, he fell back on the prominent text he knew by heart, the one called the Charm of the Camel, or as the Bedouins call it, Hirz al-Naqa, which is a supplication women sing over people with all kinds of illnesses. Ahmed loved its rhyming as much as he loved its curative powers, and he loved the beautiful voices of the women as much as its awesome words of anger and vengeance.

> In the Name of Allah the Merciful.
> There is no god but Him. I say it in faith and in Islam.
> And God is the greatest and I admit his greatness. There is no
> power but from God the highest and the greatest. I surrender
> to His will and let Him take charge of me. Praise and respect
> to the Lord. The creations of the heavens and of earth are far
> greater than the creations of people, but most of the people
> do not know.
> I took and blinded and pulled out the eyes of the evil man,
> and bent his head with force and pushed it between his legs
> and drew the vicious circle of Evil around him. God and owner
> of the frown of a frowner! God of a burning flame! God of the
> living and of the dead! God of the heat and the cold! God of

the green and the brown! God of the wet and the dry! God of
dark night and shooting stars! God of infinite oceans!

I beg you to bounce back the evil eye of the evil man onto
him, his family, his children, his body, and eyes, and all of the
things that he holds the dearest. And to keep doing it until he
turns into dead meat, ground meat running blood, and to do
with his belongings the same.

Who created the seven heavens alike? You see no
incongruity in the creation of the Beneficent. Then look
again: Can you see any disorder? Then turn the eye again
and again—thy look will return to thee confused when it is
fatigued.

I take refuge in God from the evil eyes of the evil man
and the tongues of the evil-tongued. I take refuge in God
from the evil of all evil men, from Satan and the magician. I
take refuge from the eye of the admirer and the jealous eye. I
take refuge in Allah from the black eye, the big eye, the blue
eye and the one-eyed. I take refuge from the eye that empties
houses and fills cemeteries. The friendly eye, the envious and
bad eye are alike.

By God, I take refuge from all animals and people that are
under your control. My God is on the righteous path. Their
evil plans shall not hurt me for God knows everything they
plan, say, and do.

In the name of God, who is enough as my protector. In
the name of God, who cures me. In the name of God, who
rehabilitates me. In the name of God, in whose name nothing
shall hurt, in earth or in heaven. He hears and he is all-knowing.
No power, except that of God, the highest and the greatest.

And those who disbelieve would almost smite you with
their eyes when they hear the Reminder, and they say: Surely
he is mad! And it is naught but a Reminder for the nations.

When he finished, Ahmed reached slowly into the leather
holster for his Swiss knife, one of the prized, expensive ones
known as a 108. A Bedouin without a knife is helpless, and Ahmed
never left home without this precious possession, which had only
one function, cutting efficiently and quickly.

To stop the poison from reaching the rest of his body, Ahmed tore a small piece from his turban and made a tight tourniquet at the base of his hand. Poison is driven by demons and so is said to spread seven times quicker than water or any other fluids. It goes directly to the brain, whispering bad energy into every cell and broadcasting the feeling to the rest of the body. A Bedouin knows better than anyone that his head is like the father in a family: it gives orders to the rest of the body, and if it's owned by a demon by means of poison, then the rest of the body will readily accept enslavement. Ahmed had no doubt that the snake was a demon in disguise, and injecting the poison was just the first step in its comprehensive evil plan to take him, his family, and his camels down.

What had he done that a demon was coming after him? He'd never asked for trouble; he'd never spit on the northwest side of his tent, nor thrown out spent tea leaves, nor stepped over an old firepit, nor crossed a graveyard after sunset, nor gone to sleep without saying his prayers. But he knew, too, that it's useless to wonder why something has happened, when what is needed is immediate action, and when the punishment very likely is being visited based on offenses known only to the punisher.

He tightened the tourniquet around his forearm until his fingers were about to pop. It was painful, and yet he never felt the pain in the middle of it. Using his other hand and his toes, he opened the knife. He blew a quick prayer on the cutting edge. He laid his hand on his foot with the bitten finger sticking out. He filled his mouth with the end of his turban, held the knife high, and smashed the blade against the base of his bitten finger with all the vigor and quickness he could muster. The finger flew away as the blood gushed out. He would need to find it later, but for the moment he couldn't see at all; it was as if a thick, warm cloud had buried his face. His head felt light; he wanted so much to lie down and sleep, but he knew he couldn't let that happen. He put down the knife and gave himself a couple of good smacks on both cheeks, until he came back to himself. He'd learned that pain can only be mitigated with even more pain somewhere else in the body.

He removed the tourniquet, letting it bleed some more to get rid of the bad blood that was contaminated by the poison. Then he wrapped the sticky, dirty cloth tightly around the cut, and held it hard. He allowed himself to lie down to absorb the pain and let it go into the ground. No doubt Monsieur Dr. Kaufmann would have found this process nonhygienic, if not a flat-out crime against his profession. But Ahmed didn't need to care about those kinds of things for the moment. French doctors think they have it all figured out; for a Bedouin, the more he knows, the more he realizes how little he knows. And besides, direct contact with sand is known to cure the incurable.

Ahmed needed some time for his blood to calm down and center itself, for he had made it very angry when he interfered with its flow. He wiped his burning eyes, satisfied before Allah that he hadn't cried. There would be no shame in it if he had, because there was no one to witness it and report it. But his grandmother had taught him that he should never show less respect for himself than he would for others, and he should never have secrets, because sooner or later they will show up on his face. *No matter what secret you have, people always find it out, even if you think they won't,* said the poem she had taught him. No, he would neither sleep nor surrender to his demonic enemy by showing emotion: he would live like a Bedouin and die like a Bedouin, regardless of who was watching.

The pain was starting to dissipate, and the good feeling of defeating the demons washed over him. Ahmed stood up and brushed away the sand that was stuck to the side of his face with the sweat from his pain. His injured hand was still shaking, missing its severed part, and so he turned his attention to finding it. It would take the hand some time to grieve and find a peaceful closure. He collected the finger and wrapped it in another torn piece of cloth, to give it a proper burial later, with the prayer for the departed.

The worst thing about snakes is that they serve most of the time as vessels of the devil. Ahmed knew this because so many people in the camp had witnessed it. People start to hallucinate soon after the bite, and when Ahmed found himself not just riding in but driving a speeding truck, his voice screaming like the motor and his hand shifting gears, he had conclusive proof that a mean demon was involved. People hate snakes, and God knows they have their reasons, but Ahmed knew snakes don't want to bite people, and neither do they enjoy it. Snakes bite out of the need to free themselves of the burden of the devil by passing it on and injecting it into another being.

Ahmed took a little bit of Zero, a multipurpose Chinese ointment he kept with him at all times, and applied it beneath the cloth. There was hardly any ailment that Zero couldn't cure. He had great respect for Chinese doctors, much more than the French, for the Chinese can make medications for ailments they've never seen. The healing process had begun when the thorn was pulled out, as the Bedouins say. For the next few days he would have to apply his camel's high-quality urine to help the injury close and heal, and wait. If he felt the throbbing pain running up and down his arm, he would know the poison had made it to the heart. God forbid! That would be the end.

Knowing that thinking about bad things can attract them, he tried to think about a bright future that saw him bringing Zarga back and cherishing the happiness on his son's face. "Wish for the good to find it!" his grandmother would tell him when he was upset as a child. "Allah will provide for you as long as you have faith and trust." It was as al-Mutanabbi wrote:

> Big things happen when big people will them,
> And big donations come from generosity rather than wealth.
> In the eyes of the small one, small things are big,
> But big things are small in the eyes of the big hearted.

The blood started to clot, the bleeding stopped, and the pain slowly started to ease. Relief overwhelmed him, because he knew pain is like a camel: when it starts moving away, it does so steadily and quickly.

He took a couple of sips from his guirbah. Without raw liver to replace the blood, he needed any kind of liquid, the thicker and redder the better, but at the very least water. Ahmed was not the kind of man who would waste water, and he had learned to make a very little water last over very long distances. But now he felt thirsty like never before. This came as no surprise, since demons are known to suck the juice of life out of a person as soon they enter the body through poison. By getting rid of the poisoned finger, he had not given them enough time to finish their evil.

Feeling safer now, Ahmed went back to sleep. A snake never bites twice in the same day, and the snake that bit him would have spread the news among its peers not to waste more poison on the same person.

6

THE PAIN had eased, but his dreams were fevered. A pack of hungry dogs attacked him, large long-legged dogs with big black snouts. Their mouths were open at all times, and they didn't pant like regular dogs. They were grayish, sprinkled all over with small white spots. They were talking to one another in an indistinct chatter, as if they were whispering about him, which naturally made him uncomfortable. He hated it when people whispered about him in his presence! As he tried to run away, he discovered his feet were welded to solid ground with a very thick chain emanating from a dirty, rusty manhole, like the unsanitary, overflowing, stinking manholes he'd seen in the city he visited as a child.

One of the dogs approached, its mouth wide open. He tried to fend him off by hiding his face behind his bent arm, his elbow exposed as an apparent offering to the attacking beast. As horrific as it would be to sacrifice an arm to the beast, he had to keep his face untouched, because if he were to lose his eyes, it would be practically impossible to get to safety.

He put his offered arm all the way into the mouth of the first dog, and the dog took it and crushed it. He could feel the beast's cold teeth: it was over. He readied his body for the worst, waiting for the pain from his crushed bones. To his surprise, except for a light pressure around his arm and the oddly pleasant, slowly warming feeling of the teeth, he didn't feel anything. But the intense pressure on his arm was terrifying. The pain would come when the dog released the arm, he thought, when the blood would gush and he would pass out from the sight as his soul drained out along with his blood.

He jerked his arm away, escaping from the hungry beast with just an angry bite mark. But this was only one dog, not even the biggest or meanest in the pack, which kept growing and growling. He now saw the hopelessness of his situation and the impossibility of fighting off so many attacking dogs with no one watching his back. Even worse, the pack of dogs started to be mixed up with naked people who looked like them, until there were no more dogs around; even the one that bit him was now a human. He was not comforted by this. His mother had told him that evil humans are worse than evil animals. He tried to argue with her that evil was evil, but she explained that animals would only harm him if they believed he was a threat to them, while evil humans might attack even if he did not threaten them.

"Get out!" the pack of wild human dogs kept yelling at him. "You're trespassing!"

As a child Ahmed used to be afraid of death, because his grandmother told him that sinners would be punished severely after they died and that it was very easy to sin, even unintentionally. The older he got, the less afraid of death he'd become, which seemed counterintuitive, since inevitably death gets closer with age. But he had learned over the years to justify his actions, even the ones his grandmother would consider sinful.

Still, even in his dreams he did not see death on his calendar in the near future; it was one of the things he'd rather postpone. For how long? Everyone ultimately dies, but especially the old, and he hoped to wait until he joined that category. He wanted to raise and marry off his children before he passed on to what he hoped would be a better life in the afterlife. There, he would request to work with camels—it was what he enjoyed here, so why not in the hereafter?—and prepare for his children to join him after very long and happy lives.

Out of options and cut off from any help or tools to fight off his vicious attackers, Ahmed could feel his heart expanding and pounding heavily, as if trying to fly out of his mouth. As he was watching the beasts and waiting to see himself vanish one piece at a time, he felt a wind of sadness covering him. How desolate Abdallahi and Jamila would be when they learned of his passing! A young man whose body couldn't even be found! How long would they wait until the elders told them that the man they'd loved and cherished should be considered dead? Would it be when someone found his wandering camel, saddled but with no rider? That would be conclusive evidence for everyone in the camp, because they knew that Ahmed would never leave Laamesh alone, and that Laamesh would never abandon him.

The thought of Laamesh terrified him. He looked around wildly, but he couldn't find his camel anywhere. That puzzled him, since he'd taken all precautions to keep him near. But Laamesh had disappeared from the earth, the pack of attackers was gone, and Ahmed now found himself alone, a tiny speck of sand in the vast desert.

The loss of a second camel was too much. He tried to cry: even a hardened nomad couldn't hold out in that situation. But he couldn't find any tears. He was dry-crying with his heart, until the burning in his eyes and the hoarseness in his throat hurt so much he could cry for real. It was relief achieved through pain.

Going on without his camel would be suicide, he knew. He did not know how he would survive the journey home, either, but he started walking in that direction. Miracles don't come through deliberate and careful consideration. Miracles are set in motion only when a Bedouin's idea starts to be put into practice. Of all the verses his grandmother had taught him, the one he held closest was this:

> Indeed, Allah will not change the condition of a people until they change what is in themselves.

47

The warmth of the morning sun woke him. He sat up, shaken, and reached for his bait, the leather wallet that held his bone pipe and tobacco, the cleaning rod, the flintstone, the flint iron, and old burning wool. He took out the pipe and tapped its head to get rid of the ashes. He looked inside it and sucked the cold stem, but the pipe was still congested, so he took out the cleaning rod and ran it in and out, and then blew and sucked on the cold pipe in turn to clear the resin. He hit the pipe against his heel, rubbing the resin on the back of his leg to ward off desert bugs and scorpions, and he put a little bit of it on the open wound. The burning pain almost made him pass out. Finally, he filled the pipe and held the tobacco in place with his left palm, then took out a small piece of the wool with his other hand. He pressed the wool against the flintstone with his left thumb, and, taking the flint iron in his right hand, he struck the flintstone over and over until the sparks took hold and the wool smoked. The smell was both sweet and familiar. He held the smoking wool between his right thumb and index finger and slowly pushed it against the tobacco in the mouth of his pipe, sucking on the stem to ignite it.

Ahmed performed all of this automatically; when his body needed a smoke, his hands moved and provided. His missing finger didn't seem to slow him down that much, and he knew he would be fully used to it sooner rather than later. He'd seen many Bedouins lose a part of their body without it really affecting their lives. On some level, he was proud he'd lost his finger in an honorable way, and by his own choosing.

He inhaled deeply and freely. Smoking was largely a solitary pleasure for Ahmed, since it was generally frowned upon in camp. Though men could smoke in front of older women, and some older men would even invite their sons to smoke around them, Ahmed had never disrespected his elders by blowing smoke in their presence. There had been one moment of embarrassment when he found himself preparing his pipe in front of an elder without realizing what he was doing. It was months before he could face that old man and talk to him as he had before.

And yet he also understood the other side of this taboo: in fact, a man of his age and time who didn't smoke was not to be trusted. "Does he smoke?" was one of the first things a Bedouin would ask about someone he had just met, in order to know his personality. Those who didn't smoke because of religion or other reasons set themselves apart from their peers, and so, ironically, people naturally mistrusted them, as they mistrusted all prudish people. All Bedouins are fallible, and the more one realized and made peace with this, the more one was accepted and trusted. And so something frowned upon was also embraced, and something that was forbidden was also a fabric of the culture. It was only when the French came with their smelly, illicit cigarettes that this balance was corrupted, as young people began to lose their way and smoke without taking the time to savor it and enjoy the moment.

He felt good after the second drag, and deeply inhaled the smoke again. If Ahmed had said the fresh morning breeze was not better than a deep drag of high-quality tobacco, he would not be lying. He wiped his hands on the sand, which was still very cool from the night air, and rubbed them lightly all over his face in a ritual before his morning prayer. He should have said the prayer the first thing in the morning, but he might not have been able to stand up straight without his tobacco.

As he performed his prayer, he thought he heard Laamesh grumbling not far away, and beyond that human voices. When he was finished, he grabbed his guirbah and set off to find him. Hobbled, he wouldn't be far. And Laamesh was a good boy; he understood that Ahmed needed him. He knew Ahmed needed to get to the next Bedouin camp and center himself with a hot cup of thick, well-brewed green tea. Ahmed had learned to take everything life threw at him with grace and acceptance, but he didn't deal well with the headache that came when he didn't get his cup of tea. It was his weak point, he would admit, but he would never apologize for it. A man needs his cup of tea.

A blind man could have followed the animal's hoofprints on the quiet sand. Ahmed soon spotted Laamesh in a valley below the small hill where he'd spent the night. He was breakfasting on the branches of a tree, meticulously fighting through the sharp thorns to get to the scarce leaves with his big and flexible snout.

Laamesh looked at his owner with the side of his eye and smiled. Some may doubt that camels smile, but to Ahmed this wasn't up for debate. He had seen camels smiling and heard them talking, laughing, and of course crying. But no one could doubt the crying: even the most cynical can hear it, as loud and as clear as the whispers of a jinn family when darkness falls.

Laamesh greeted Ahmed by lowering his head and allowing him to untie the tether. Together, they started toward the voices Ahmed had been hearing.

Soon he stood in front of the first tent and greeted its inhabitants.

> Salamu Alaikum!
> Waalaikum Salam!
> What's new?
> Thank God, nothing! What's new?

When the Bedouin greetings and small talk dwindled, Ahmed invited himself inside. In the desert, three days in a strange tent is your right. After the three days, a host can ask you to move on, though Ahmed had never heard of anyone doing this, because everyone knows that the host is merely a proxy between the guest and Allah, and it's only Satan who whispers otherwise. And thank God it's that way; otherwise no one would survive.

The man of the tent handed him a cup of fresh-brewed green tea, his favorite, the gunpowder kind, made in China. It smelled sweet and strong, and Ahmed hoped it was the first round of a three-round tea session. Nobody wants to miss the thickness and concentration of the first brewed round, and only the first brew could fix Ahmed's brick-heavy head after the punishment he'd been through. He took a quick, loud sip, then held the cup tight between his fingers, feeling the warmth creeping up his hand, into his arm, and all the way to his brain. He allowed the steam into his nose, loudly inhaling, knowing it was the shortcut into a very tired brain, and deliberately squeezed the cup against the wound to help sharpen his senses.

The glass hadn't been washed from the last time its owner had made tea, which gave it an extra aroma; in the way people elsewhere like aged wine, people in this part of the world like tea that has an old taste to it. There was sand in it as well; in this part of the desert it is hard to find a sip without some clean sand in it. A little sand won't hurt anybody. When he took the first sip, his eyes grew wide. The eyes can only see what the head wants them to see, and Ahmed's head had focused his eyes on what he needed to see to survive. Now he started to see things that he hadn't seen before, and he knew he was safe and in good hands.

His heart was filled with joy and optimism. It was one of those moments he wished he could freeze in time and hold until he passed away. He imagined that paradise would be filled with moments like these, when your heart would be satisfied and at peace. We only recognize things by contrast; safety can be understood only when you experience its absence, and joy can be appreciated only if you've been through pain and suffering. And yes, you really appreciate your camel the way you should only if you lose it. Ahmed was certainly not a learned philosopher, but he knew this much from his grandmother, and from the school of life, where no theory is allowed and where you can only pass a test after failing it many times over.

The next sips seemed to defy gravity and climb straight to his head. And then a last loud sip declared the end of the cup. He both loved and hated the last sip the most. It tasted better than the rest, and was much easier to swallow because it was just warm enough to please the throat. Yes, he could have put his teacup down and waited until the whole cup cooled, but then he wouldn't have been drinking, and this way made the last sip even more perfect and bittersweet. He tried not to repeat the saying that always came to mind at this moment: All good things have an end. Why remind oneself of this in the middle of such enjoyment?

"What did Allah name you?" The host's question cut through Ahmed's deep train of thoughts, shaking him out of his satisfied self-hypnosis.

"Ahmed Ould Abdallahi, from the tribe of Idamoor," Ahmed responded. His voice was low, though not too low to hide the pride when he mentioned his tribe.

"Beautiful reputation you have!" his host commented. "My name is Omar Ould Sidi." He looked toward his guest with the sides of his eyes while unwrapping a big bar of hard sugar and breaking off a decent piece with the bottom of a tea glass. He added the piece to the pot, cradling the bar as he would a small child and making sure to pick up every trace that had fallen and adding it to the teapot. Nothing must go to waste. "This camp belongs to the tribe of Awladhoum," he continued.

"Beautiful reputation you have!" Ahmed answered automatically but emphatically, not caring too much for the weight his words were carrying. A word's weight diminishes every time you utter it, until it comes to a point where it has no more weight to lose. These words of praise, they both knew, were hardly words at all, but tokens of peace and trust. No further introductions were necessary; with time, the guest would get to know the other members of his host's family.

Ahmed deliberately did not speak of his ordeal the night before with the possessed snake. It was a story about him, and not in his favor. He took full responsibility for the recklessness that led to his being bitten. For a man of the desert, when something bad happens to him, the fault is always his. But when the lady of the house handed him a bowl of fresh milk, her eyes landed for a moment on the fresh wound and missing finger. Ahmed knew she was seeing a man who'd been through distressing times.

"Fatima," she introduced herself simply. "What happened to you?" she asked, smiling. A Bedouin woman tends to skip the courtesies that are prevalent in city life, to the benefit of her honesty and true care for her guests.

Ahmed took the bowl. As he tipped it to his lips he glanced around the tent, measuring his hosts' humble circumstances. He took the usual three loud sips, but then he drank just enough to balance out the aggressiveness of the green tea on his empty stomach, and returned the bowl. He didn't thank her in any explicit way, but his behavior conveyed the sort of kindness that is buried in the heart and waits for the right opportunity to be expressed in ways other than overused small talk. Fatima and Ahmed both understood that he was thankful.

Ahmed was torn between satisfying his hosts and allowing himself to grieve and deal with his pain in private. He took some time before addressing the lady's question. Finally he looked at her and told her about his encounter with the evil snake. He tried to downplay his bravery and the seriousness of the encounter.

As he was talking he pulled the part of his turban that covered his chin over his mouth. It was a habit he'd developed as a young man, when he was self-conscious about losing the first of his permanent teeth. He had lost many more over the years, and cared much less what people thought. But the covering still felt warm and comfortable, and let him concentrate on telling the story with the right balance of detail and modesty. He had come to understand the words of the poem his old grandmother had taught him:

> Your tongue you should curb and keep in place
> And don't let it wildly run
> For everyone has that mighty piece
> And no one's perfect, even my own son.

As Ahmed spoke, Omar emptied a full glass of tea back into the teapot to give the tea a good mix. The layer of foam grew, as if the tea leaves, too, were absorbing Ahmed's story.

7

"I HAPPENED to cross the trail of that snake," Omar offered. "And the way it slithered through the sand told me that she was up to no good. It was three days ago." It was very important to a man like Omar to be precise and have a memory that was beyond reproach. In the treacherous desert, where one's life depends so completely on others, one can't afford to give or receive doubtful information. For a Bedouin seeking a stray animal or the next point of water, a reckless or inaccurate story could be as dangerous as a deliberate lie. And those who mislead unintentionally, though not outright shamed like those who lie, suffer a loss of reputation that is hard to restore. In the end a lie, for a Bedouin, is any statement that contradicts the facts, regardless of the speaker's intention.

Fatima shyly added that Sharifa Nounou, a local hajjaba, hair stylist, and amateur wedding singer, had spotted the same snake trying to sneak into the camp a couple of days earlier in the guise of a mean, blue-eyed black cat. She shooed her away, but spotted her footprints the next day, leaving the camp. Nounou decided to trail her, following the paw prints until they melted seamlessly into the continuous line of a slithering snake very much like the one Ahmed had just described.

Metamorphoses like this filled the stories Bedouins told around a tea fire at night. Ahmed never knew whether to believe them, but now the evidence pointed toward a clear-cut case of a demon intervening to disrupt a peaceful life. Though he would not let it show, Ahmed had never felt prouder of himself. His

pride was not only for him, but for every Bedouin who had suffered pain at the hands of a dishonest demon that was too much
of a coward to reveal itself and hid instead behind a snake, making the snake look like the evildoer—and for every Bedouin who
would suffer this pain in the future. The war against the forces
of evil would go on long after him, until the end of time. It was
not like a traditional fight against another tribe. It was a vicious,
asymmetrical war against an invisible, uncooperative, and un-
speaking enemy, and the Bedouins knew they were outnumbered
and outgunned. A Bedouin may live sixty or seventy years, but
a demon lives for thousands of years, and a midsized family of
demons produces seven hundred and seventy-seven offspring. A
snake is a snake, and God knows it's bad enough to be bitten by
one. But a possessed snake is a wholly different matter.

"Don't you think he should talk to Sharifa Nounou, just to be
on the safe side?" Fatima asked her husband, looking at Ahmed
with the side of her eyes to see his reaction. Fatima was emptying
the rest of the milk bowl into a skin shikwah to extract butter and
turn the skimmed milk into buttermilk. She rocked the shikwah
as she poured, sometimes slow, sometimes fast, varying the speed
by instinct and feeling. It was a process that separated righteous
adults from the rest, since only the righteous ones could pour
from a big and clumsy bowl into the tiny mouth of a shikwah.
Once her hands were freed from the awkwardness of pouring
the milk, she suggested again, with more emphasis, "We cannot
possibly let him go without consulting her."

"It's always the surest thing to do in such situations, to elimi-
nate any probable fallout, especially problems of a demonic
nature," Omar agreed, quietly but firmly. Although he did not
plan to follow their advice, Ahmed had no doubt his hosts were
right. Hajjabas like Sharifa Nounou had met and spoken to the
departed and reported it publicly on more than one occasion, or
had encountered ghosts, jinn, or even demons and given accurate
descriptions which wise men and women had been able to check

against known facts. Lying about these things would be almost inconceivable for a Bedouin. Why should anyone lie about such things, when the evidence of these beings was so overwhelmingly reported in the accounts of the elders?

Ahmed nodded as he hungrily inhaled the last sip of the second round of this cup, making the sound that announced there was no more tea left. He wished and he longed for more tea out of that cup. The middle round, the second and tastiest one, represents the proverbial golden mean, neither too strong, like the first one, nor too weak, like the last one. The cup had been poured only two-thirds full, according to etiquette; less suggested a guest was not truly welcome, and more was regarded as too familiar and inappropriate.

Looking at Omar, Ahmed removed his turban completely to use as a pillow and placed it under his bent right leg. It was a sign he felt welcome and relaxed in the tent of his hosts. Two well-brewed cups of green tea would be enough to convince even the most hardened cynic that everything was okay, and that the hospitality was real and genuine.

Fatima took a very old and overused pillow she had been using herself and tossed it to Ahmed to add to the turban. Ahmed was no brat, and would never have asked, but the straw mat was too rough to lie on without the second pillow, and he accepted it gratefully.

"We lost her yesterday, a young two-and-a-half-year-old camel. She's blue." Ahmed offered the description of his stray camel, ignoring his hosts' proposal that he seek medical and spiritual attention. He knew very well the danger of being visited again by the evil spirits. A second attack would be worse and harder to ward off, since the spirit would be armed with the knowledge it had gained from the first attack. But Zarga might now be in peril, and she was his highest priority. He'd given himself more than enough attention already and wasn't planning on wasting his time on patching himself up further. That would be bordering on obsession, or even worse, vanity, a trait worse than the bite of an evil snake.

Omar stoked the tea fire, which was starting to choke beneath a thickening layer of dead ash. "We haven't seen any stray camels in any of the neighboring herds. But yesterday I saw a sea of camels that was being driven westward, rather hurriedly. In all likelihood, they could be heading to Dakhla or beyond." Pressing his left nostril with his left thumb and turning away from his guest, in accordance with custom, he cleared his nose unselfconsciously. "From what I've heard, the herds belong to a renowned Moroccan tribe that moves inside our country sometimes for fresh and untouched grazing ground," Omar continued, the words emerging from one side of his mouth while the other side sucked hard on the dying fire in his big wet pipe. He tapped the pipe lightly with his right index finger to push the ash inside. His gestures and manners were cautious and unobtrusive. "I wouldn't be surprised if your camel was mopped up along with them. Maybe even on purpose. Those people never shy away from cleaning up as they leave the country and head home."

Omar paused and looked straight at his guest. "I hope I'm wrong. Otherwise you'd better hurry, before your camel starts to learn a new language," he added, his eyes widening for emphasis.

Ahmed's emotions were boiling at the thought. Zarga belonged to home, not Morocco, and to home she should return. But his Bedouin instincts told him the scenario was plausible. Omar went on to tell him where he'd seen the herds. Ahmed would only have to cross the path he described and quickly study some hoofprints to know he had the right camels. Every country has a different kind of sand, and that sand defines the shape of the prints as the baby camel trains itself to walk. From that point on, Ahmed would be able to track the herd properly. In their last stage, when the herd is heading back home and the herder doesn't need to look for fresh grazing, long drives generally follow a straight line. Omar explained the likely campsites for the herders on their way back to Morocco, as well as the scarce water sources he'd encounter. He seemed to offer all this casually, but both men knew the information meant life or death to Ahmed, who would soon be venturing alone over unknown and unforgiving territory.

8

WITHOUT ANY announcement, Fatima left the tent. She came back soon with Sharifa Nounou. Ahmed understood that Fatima was looking after the safety of her family and the camp: having an evil demon roaming around and preying on innocents by taking different guises was not something she could allow. Ahmed would be within his rights to refuse to consult a spiritual hajjab, but not when other people could be hurt. It would be like someone with chickenpox refusing the usual treatment of four burns in places prescribed by a qualified hajjab, and then not drinking the milk of a donkey.

Sharifa Nounou, as her name suggested, claimed to be a direct descendant of the holy family of our Prophet, and given the things she could do and see, no one had reason to doubt her claim. She was tall—five foot six—and a handsome four hundred pounds. That was overweight even by Bedouin standards, but her weight didn't prevent her from walking as a Bedouin lady should, swaying from one side to the other, as if relieving one leg at a time by shifting her weight to the other side. In her early fifties, she should have been more mobile, but she had chosen to work less and cure more, to the detriment of her health. She also liked her food; it was one of her many vices. Her prayer-bead chain was a full nine hundred ninety-nine beads long, instead of the standard ninety-nine, and she put it to constant good use. Even when she laid it aside, her fingers would move in a quick, seizure-like motion, as though trying to push the beads down.

She wore a thick black veil. A big silver bracelet with geometrical inscriptions wrapped her left wrist, and her right was looped twice with a loose chain of smaller wooden prayer beads. A third loop wouldn't have fit around her thick wrist.

She sat down with some difficulty on the edge of the straw mat, fighting gravity the whole way. She started by bending over, hands propped on her knees, as if to perform the ritual of bowing to the ground in prayer. Then she lowered her big lower back and settled, just the way a camel would. Ahmed could only imagine how miserable this woman would be, and how impossible such maneuvers would be, had she not been praying five times a day. But Nounou's movements also showed hints of the big, beautiful, agile woman she once had been: a bullet would shake her but wouldn't break her, as the Bedouins say.

Sharifa Nounou unwrapped the small prayer beads from her wrist and started working this strand, too. Fatima ushered Ahmed closer to the hajjaba so she could take a good look at his injury. He put his turban back on, suppressing his self-consciousness in front of a woman he'd never met before. She was a professional, and he had learned long ago to respect professionals, as long as they stuck to their callings. Sharifa Nounou took Ahmed's left hand and asked him to clench it gently. With one hand she opened his hand slowly, one finger at a time, and then she closed it and opened it all at once. With her other hand she continued playing with the small prayer beads.

She didn't remove the dressing Ahmed had put on. There was no need to; it was a strict policy of hers to respect all kinds of medicine. If Ahmed had asked, she would have told him all medicine is good, even French medicine. The human body has many illnesses, some of which doctors haven't uncovered yet, and any medication you take will hit some illness and start fighting it.

Sharifa Nounou's expertise lay not in fighting bacterial infection, a mundane job that can be done by almost anyone with minimal training. She had seen harmless injuries cure themselves, without any human intervention. No, Sharifa Nounou was out on her own, carrying out her own kind of jihad, going after much more sinister forces. Cynical people denied this unseen world, but when they got caught in it they would beg her for help. The biggest mistake you can make in a war is to underestimate your enemy, and the biggest way to underestimate your enemy is not to recognize that it exists. But no matter how often she warned people to take these forces seriously, many still fell victim through their cynicism.

Sharifa Nounou was well prepared herself. The biggest weapon in her arsenal was her long chain of prayer beads. For all the ailments she'd ever encountered, she had mastered a specific watertight and tested standard operating procedure. And yet every time she performed that ritual, she discovered new angles that required endless improvisations and variations.

For snakebite laced with demon spit, she asked the lady of the house to bring her a strong thread, a knife, and a small branding rod. She took the thread, and with Fatima's help she measured out the length from her bent elbow to the tip of her middle finger. She did this demonstratively, waving her arm up and down and looking at everyone to call them to witness and take note of the measurement. A hajjaba's reputation depends on people trusting in her process, and because so much of the process must take place away from the public's eyes, she will work even harder to ensure that everyone can see the visible parts.

Ahmed could see that her self-confidence was unshakable. Clearly she wasn't doing this ritual for the first time. The stern look on her face bespoke the kinds of demons she had dealt with in her career. As much as he hated the attention and the waste of precious time, Ahmed was happy he was in the hands of this wise woman.

Sharifa Nounou began to mumble some prayers Ahmed had never heard before. She spoke too quickly and softly for him to make them out. This was deliberate: hajjabas don't want people to pick up their prayers. They especially fear children, who memorize more quickly than old people since their brains aren't yet dried up by the hot sun. Their greatest responsibility is to keep their prayers and supplications secret. Theirs is not a job for the fainthearted, and there is a price to pay for knowing these things. Sharifa herself had paid it. She had no children. She had paid it willingly, though. She needed to protect her community from the vengeful retaliation of evil spirits. This meant teaching her community how to deal with the unseen world without provoking it. It also meant, whenever an opportunity presented itself, explaining to the spirits that her people never meant to hurt them.

Invisible spirits are invisible to us either because our eyesight is weak or because we just don't care enough to pay attention and see beyond our preconceived notions. But the spirits believe we see them and act against them on purpose. Few on either side know that most of our unfortunate encounters happen by accident and misunderstanding. Sharifa Nounou had the difficult task of trying to bring these very different worlds together to live in peace and harmony. If both parties came to understand each other, Sharifa Nounou would be without a job. But that was impossible. Despite her efforts, the conflict would be as alive on the day of her passing as when the first demon tribe landed from a foreign planet.

During her prayers and supplications, she kept swinging her right fist, which held the thread, and tapping her shoulders with the prayer beads. After every prayer she would blow lightly into her palm, allowing tiny drops of saliva to touch the rod. She tapped lightly with the string on his injured hand.

With Fatima's help, she measured out the length again, and this time, Ahmed was not surprised to see, the thread was shorter. The next time around, the thread was longer. Right before his eyes, like a magician doing card tricks, she would tap his hand and make the measurement, with a different result every time.

Ahmed was no cynic, and he tended to believe what people told him, as long as they proved to be decent and showed religious reverence. But for a few moments his curiosity and his drive to know got the better of him, and a small shade of doubt crept into his heart. He tried to figure out if she was cheating—if she was holding her side of the thread, perhaps, which would explain the shrinking. But he couldn't see how she could make it longer. He quickly felt guilty about his heart's behavior and silently made amends. After all, he couldn't hope to be cured if he didn't believe in the cure; his grandmother had taught him that cynics can't be healed. By believing in your healer, you give permission to your body to open up and deploy its own army to chase the bad spirits away. Everyone knows this! Most certainly, Sharifa Nounou was only trying to help her guest and had not done anything to deserve his mistrust.

Healing, he reminded himself, is to be received blindly, unquestioningly. The worst that could happen was that the cure wouldn't work, and that was okay; no one, Ahmed included, would suggest that a healer should always be successful. The process was at best hit-and-miss, with more misses than hits, and its success depended on both the healer and the healed. To doubt the process and question the integrity of his healer was to risk being cursed by the healer, and that was a price Ahmed was not ready to pay.

As Ahmed was drowning in his inner thoughts, Sharifa Nounou was taking care of her job, doing the same measurements over and over, tapping her hand and looking at those around her for silent approval. She kept checking and rechecking the process to show that she wasn't missing anything. The smirk on her face betrayed her self-satisfaction. The thread continued shrinking and expanding. Unseen forces were clearly tampering with it, which was both bad and good news. The bad news was obvious. The good news was that these forces seemed to be under Sharifa's medical spell.

Now that Sharifa Nounou had confirmed the presence of those evil forces, Ahmed knew, in hindsight, that something had been wrong with him even before the snakebite. Some evil eye had stricken him long ago, and the snakebite merely added salt to an old wound. Now Ahmed started to see Nounou's power and proficiency. The light of the morning sun suddenly filled his eyes. He felt very small before this big woman, not just physically but spiritually. And the doubt he had felt when she first started tapping his hand with the thread made him feel smaller yet. His grandmother had taught him that saying something bad about someone, even to yourself, will give that person the power to be better than you.

After each measurement, Sharifa Nounou tied a knot at a seemingly random spot along the thread. She repeated the process exactly seven times; any more would damage the process and require it to be postponed to another day. Such rituals, as everybody knows, cannot be repeated the same day. When the thread had seven knots, she wrapped it around Ahmed's wrist, making a loose bracelet. "You should not remove this bracelet for the next seven days, under any circumstances," she said sternly, looking in Ahmed's eyes to make sure he understood. He felt goosebumps running over his whole body like a fire over dry grass. A current swept through him, and his temples and forehead started to sweat, although the morning was still cool with last night's dew. A wave of goodness freed the dark grip on his spine, overwhelming his body like cold water on a hot day.

Sharifa Nounou put the tip of the small iron rod in the tea fire and waited for it to glow red. She laid Ahmed on his side and asked Fatima and her husband to hold him tightly. This next step didn't require Ahmed's consent; he had already agreed to it the moment he let Sharifa Nounou cast the first good spell on him. She gave him a small, round burn just above the ankle of the leg opposite the injured hand. The pain of the injured side had to be balanced out by a pain of similar magnitude, eliminating the soul's confusion and putting it at peace. Though she was quick, the pain was immense, and his leg jerked involuntarily. His eyes watered a little, and he stuck his face in the sand lest someone see him, especially the women. The sand made him choke, but he was glad no one could read his expression or see the tears. But it was no shame that his leg jerked violently; that happens even to strong camels when they're branded.

The burn was a precautionary measure in case the charm failed to cover everything, a way for Sharifa Nounou to show how thorough she was. In spite of the pain, Ahmed felt much better. His hosts felt relieved, too. Not only had they helped a man in need, but they had been able to strike a blow, a much-needed preemptive strike, against an enemy that had been looming around their camp.

Sharifa Nounou, as always, asked for no compensation, saying that she did what she did for the sake of Allah. But not asking does not mean not expecting, and she did expect a small reward. Fatima put some dehydrated meat, a handful of Medina dates, and a between-two-fingers measure of tea leaves in a small wooden bowl and set it beside Sharifa Nounou. The sugar and dates evoked the sweet ending of the story, and the bitterness of the tea symbolized the defeated enemy.

Ahmed looked at Fatima with a tinge of envy, wishing he could be the one giving the gift. He would have, had he been home. It stings when you can't extend your hand in gift to others. His grandmother always repeated the messenger's saying to him:

The hand that gives is better than the hand that takes.

9

SO MANY things had happened in such a short time, between the second and the third round of tea. Now, as Ahmed sipped the remnants of his third cup, he decided it was time to leave. In keeping with Bedouin custom, he didn't thank his hosts, despite everything they had done for him. People express gratitude in other forms, like spreading good reports about those who welcomed them.

Ahmed filled his pipe for one more badly needed smoke. After the exquisite preparations, he took a single long drag and stuck the burning pipe back in his leather holster. It was a waste of good tobacco, but it was worth it. Unlike many other human beings, Bedouins will readily admit their contradictions; they know that good and evil both exist in the body, and the one they give more milk and food that day is the one that will be stronger. And after a traumatic event, nothing can fix a man like a sweet drag of his well-maintained pipe.

Ahmed would have to get moving before the baking sun reached noon, when it would hit a nomad's head like a glowing hammer. Riding through the day was not an option in the desert, and it was not realistic to think he could catch up to the herd heading west before he had to take a break. In this part of the world, a mean demon stands tall in the middle of the sky and spits fire on those who choose not to take shelter, and doesn't stop until the sun cools down enough that a mature camel can look straight at it, or a blind man can see it as a hot black spot. It would take a combination of day and night travel with very short breaks.

His plan for the day was to reach a water point that Omar had described for him called Beer Hasi. At a normal pace, he would get there when his shadow was just above one foot toward the northeast. He would water his camel, drink, and fill his guirbah with water. In such heat, nomads know not to drink pure water, which is too light for the desert heat, making it easy to sweat out. They will mix it with something, buttermilk if possible, or ground peanuts or watermelon seeds, thickening it so the body can hold onto it longer.

Ahmed went as Omar had directed, keeping the long hill on the left and following the camels' dung, the fresher the better, until the mouth of the valley tightened. Crossing the hill and leaving it on his right, he reached Beer Hasi.

This was not a place where someone would settle. The herds that had passed the day before hadn't made a stop, and Ahmed could see from the droppings around the well that the last time anyone drew any water was about two weeks ago. A well needs to have water drawn regularly to keep the fresh water coming. The closest human beings to Beer Hasi were in Omar's camp, but Omar had evidently left this task to the dwellers of nowhere, the unseen spirits, both good and bad. Only one of the two pools had water in it, and it was thick, green, and filled with all kinds of desert insects. Even Laamesh had trouble quenching his thirst from it. Ahmed took off his turban and used it to filter the water. Using the water sparingly, he filled his guirbah and washed his camel. Then he settled beneath an old tree, mixed some ground peanuts with water, and drank until he was satisfied but not full. He knew drinking water this dirty was risking the kind of stomachache that would double him over and make it difficult to pee. But a Bedouin was born to defy the harsh desert, and he would be all right as long as no fever clouded his senses and stranded him in the middle of nowhere.

Just a few miles before the water point nothing had cast a shadow. But now there was enough shade for him to lie down on the northeast side of the tree. He used part of his turban as a pillow and the smaller part to cover his face from the light, and settled down for a short rest. It was the most he could afford.

Soon he was on his way again, heading left from the water source and continuing west with a slight drift to the north. Nobody needed to tell Ahmed how to locate a nomad's camp. He needed to avoid the bigger herds, which belong to small groups of herders that cover too much ground for their herders to build full camps, and to track the smaller herds. Their trails inevitably led to a community of tents.

Fortified by the break, Laamesh covered ground quickly. Ahmed mostly rode, but occasionally dismounted to walk, leading his camel by the tether. It gave Laamesh a break from his weight and time to straighten his back and let blood flow into his legs. When they crossed a dune, Ahmed would take off his sandals so he wouldn't get stuck and fought his way over, while Laamesh's sure, flat feet floated above the sand. Toward evening, they crossed a trail of two or three camels, and Ahmed guided Laamesh in that direction. Before long he found himself scanning a camp of a dozen or so tents pitched seemingly at random, most of them made of sheep's wool.

From the size, the color, and the knitting of the tents he could clearly tell the social status of the owners. Ahmed picked the smallest tent, which likely belonged to the camp's hired herder. He always felt uneasy around rich people. He didn't understand their jokes—when they made jokes, which was rare. But among the herders and the domestic workers he felt at home. He enjoyed their simplicity, honesty, and their sense of humor, which matched his own. He had a particular liking for their crude, taboo jokes, which would offend and be misunderstood by the well-to-dos.

He knelt Laamesh before the tent and removed the saddle and the tether for the first time since he had left home, to give Laamesh as much rest as he could. Ahmed was tired, but Laamesh was even more tired, for Ahmed was the one who had been riding. He passed his hand gently over Laamesh, petting him, combing the fur with his hand to give him the look that the handsome camel deserved. He whispered a prayer of thanks into the camel's ear as he removed the tether from his piercing.

In the tent he found a lone, slender, athletic-looking woman. She had a hardworking, self-confident look to her, and when he greeted her he could see the honest welcome on her face. After the usual small talk, she said that the man of the tent, her husband Mohamed, was running late but should be home soon. It was her way of making her guest comfortable about accepting her implied invitation to step farther into the tent. But Ahmed was already at ease, trusting the instinct that had led him to the tent.

"What does Allah call you?" she asked.

"My name is Ahmed from Idamoor," he answered, volunteering the name of his tribe as well. The history of one's tribe, the wars it has fought, and the peace treaties it has forged with others are all factors that determine a tribe's standing, and Ahmed knew his tribe's reputation was very good. The Idamoor had fought wars, made peace, and resisted colonization, according to his elders, and he had no reason to believe they were lying to him. But having a good reputation in one's own territory doesn't necessarily mean that reputation has carried to other places. In this territory they might not even know his tribe. That could be both good and bad. He'd lose the advantage that came with the tribe's honor. But if he were regarded as a nobody, just another Bedouin looking for a stray camel, he could get the information he needed and avoid being grilled about who had married, who had divorced, and who had died. And he could avoid any tricky political situations involving tax collectors, if his hosts happened to be from a tribe entrusted by the French to do that job. But Ahmed intuitively trusted this woman, and he proudly declared his tribe.

"Beautiful reputation you have!" she said casually. She busied herself preparing a drink for her guest, deliberately passing up the opportunity to fish for a compliment for her own tribe. And she may not have even recognized his. She had the air of someone for whom tribe doesn't matter, someone who regarded every individual based on his or her merit—an attitude that Ahmed had encountered rarely, and almost exclusively among former slaves. It was as though, in passing from slavery to freedom, they had also been freed from the weight people place on connections or descent. Ahmed did not ask her who she was; she would come to that on her own if she was so inclined.

She tossed him the only pillow in that tent. Calling it a pillow was a stretch: it was old and dirty, with many patches already and a desperate need for more. The straw mat was in no better shape. It didn't matter to Ahmed. He winced as he shed his sandals, rubbing the angry marks they left between his long and index toes. He stretched out on the straw mat, covering his face with the end of his turban. He was asleep the moment he laid his head down on the poor, worn pillow.

10

ZARGA WAS trying to drink with the rest of a strange herd. She had wandered for a long time trying to find her family, and when she couldn't, she decided that some company was better than none. The herder kept warding her off, beating her harshly with a long thick stick to prevent her from sharing the water. The stick was laughing sardonically every time the strange herder struck her.

"I didn't mean to strike you. Why didn't you stay with your own family?" the herder was saying, but the stick was in charge. For years it had used the herder to beat his animals, and now they had come to resemble one another, the herder growing long and hard like the stick, and the stick growing a dark, thick fringe that mirrored the herder's mustache and beard.

Ahmed was watching from afar. When he tried to come to her rescue, fear and anger settled in his legs. They became so heavy he couldn't move an inch, as if he were being sucked deep into quicksand. He knelt like a camel, figuring that camels, with their four legs, never fail to walk. And being four-legged means that you can stomp people, so they are scared of you. He found he could make himself as big as he wished by taking deep breaths, as if blowing up a big balloon that was his body. And so he became very big, even bigger than the herd's biggest bull.

He was afraid for a moment that he might blow up. He tried to move forward, but his hind legs were shackled to the big tree he had visited as a child in the center of the city. But then the tree was a big Caterpillar bulldozer with thick belt tracks like the ones that he'd seen on the French military vehicles that made awesome noises and awful-smelling clouds of smoke as they drove everyone else off the road.

A real camel could defeat a French military vehicle. But the more Ahmed tried to free his legs, the more sticks fell from the sky onto his hands. They cried out as he pushed them away, and started to suck on his nipples, tickling him and undermining his efforts to break loose.

In desperation, he tried to shout and scare off the stick that was beating Zarga, not with the herder now, but with a small crying baby. He was straining to make his voice heard, if only so Zarga could see that he hadn't let her down, if only to strengthen her morale in the face of adversity and pain. Zarga was begging the stick to stop and looking everywhere for help, except in Ahmed's direction. Try as he might, he couldn't get his voice out; he was shouting into a big bubble that surrounded him. He became so hoarse he couldn't hear it himself. The ground beneath him started to sweat with warm water, like dew emanating from solid ground. The sweat covered his body, and he was choking and gasping for air.

When Zarga finally looked at him, she metamorphosed into his own son, Abdallahi. She didn't say anything now, just cried loudly in the high-pitched voice of a child. In his nightmare, Ahmed judged nothing; he just observed and accepted the events exactly as they presented themselves to him. He had turned into an all-powerful giant who could be everywhere in time and space but had the intelligence of a little baby. Zarga kept metamorphosing, shifting back and forth between herself and Abdallahi, and sometimes a mixture of both.

As Zarga was crying, the herder headed toward Ahmed with a glowing-hot rod, mistaking him for one of his camels that he was planning to brand. After all, Ahmed was standing on his four limbs. He tried to stand up on two feet to show the herder he wasn't a camel, but his hands stuck in the sand and he could not speak. To the strange herder, all signs indicated Ahmed was an animal for real, a stray animal belonging to no one, and so his to claim.

Ahmed jerked his hand away violently as he felt the approaching heat of the branding rod. He opened his eyes, looking straight at the roof of the tent, not knowing where he was or with whom. He felt so heavy and tired that he couldn't move. He realized that what he had been dreaming was a brand was a lady gently touching his hand with the edge of the hot teacup, trying to wake him. He'd seen this lady before, he thought, and then recognized she was his host. His eyes were watering. The child in the tent was crying at the top of his lungs. The heat in the tent was choking.

"Jatma threw herself on you!" the lady of the house remarked. As Ahmed came back to himself, he thanked God. Jatma is everyone's grandmother, who protects sleeping souls. She is heavy and she wears a black veil. When she feels that one of her grandchildren is about to do something dangerous in a dream, she throws herself on the child, trying to paralyze it, so the child cannot act on its intentions. It's a kind of tough love: if we try to talk, shout, hit, jump, or run, she'll paralyze us. She takes away all our voluntary actions, leaving us with the bare minimum to keep us alive, our breathing and our heart's beating and the mumbling of the necessary prayers to fend off the bad spirits. She had come to help Ahmed on many occasions, especially when he was a child, and he knew she'd never harm him. He knew a Bedouin heart can't stop beating, because it's the part of his body that encourages him to do good.

"What does Allah call you?" he asked her. "You have one angry child!" Ahmed wasn't prying, but this was a good woman and he couldn't wait to know who she was.

"My name is M'barka. My son Mohamed has recently been circumcised. He's been having problems peeing and I just applied a little bit of Hell's Breath mixed with the urine of a pregnant she-camel to his injury. It bites a little." In fact, this secret herbal mixture nomads put on fresh wounds as a disinfectant burns as badly as its name.

M'barka was clearly used to working and carrying on an important conversation at the same time. She was in the last stage of preparing zrig, buttermilk mixed with water and sugar or salt, for her guest. He was confident he could skip formalities with her altogether, for the same reason he had chosen a small tent belonging to a poor family. Nothing made him more uneasy than pretending to be someone he wasn't. To have to keep checking on his clothes, watching where his hands were, swishing his words in his mouth before uttering them for a scrutinizing audience, faking smiles, laughing at unfunny jokes, avoiding picking his itchy nose: these were the sorts of things that Ahmed hated most about dealing with complicated rich folks.

"Don't waste no sugar on my drink! I wanna drink without it, it's too precious!" Ahmed said. M'barka looked relieved. Ahmed could see this was not a family that kept provisions for a week. They lived one day at a time, with the barest minimum.

"You're after a stray camel, right?" she asked, extending her hand with the wooden bowl of zrig.

"Her name is Zarga. Two and a half years old, blue, with the spots on her head, belly, and front legs. Bearing our brand, the bent stick and the point," he said, searching M'barka's face for any sign that she had information she could reveal to him. He didn't think she was the kind of woman who wouldn't take note of men's talk around tea. "Bismillah!"

He grabbed the bowl with one hand and blew on the surface of the liquid to clear the foam that built up when she whisked it. He took a big sip, making a loud slurp.

"I believe my husband saw her last night with transiting Marrakesh troops," she said, "but I'm not sure about the details. It would be best to wait on him and ask him yourself."

Ahmed nodded. He blew lightly into the bowl again, took another slurp, and then quietly drank half of the one-and-half-liter bowl. He handed the bowl back to her and used the end of his turban to clean the sticky foam from his mustache.

The pain from the bad dream washed over his body, forcing him to lie back down. He promised himself not to fall asleep again. He didn't want to go back to the torment of the nightmare. He didn't want to see Zarga suffering anymore. And yet as soon as he lay his head on the pillow, he started to snore.

To stop his snoring from bothering her and her son, M'barka took a special string and hung it over his head between the two poles that held up the tent. As soon as his soul felt it, he stopped snoring. The string was made to scare away the demon of snoring, and luckily, the snoring demon that accompanied Ahmed seemed to be smaller and more superstitious than his peers. The more one snores, the older the demon grows and the harder it is to scare. That is why the snoring of old people is almost unstoppable.

The herder with the long stick appeared again. Ahmed took the stick away and threatened to break it if the man dared to hit his camel. The man staggered, shaken. Behind him an old man with a long gray beard and thick hair that all but covered his face opened his mouth. "In every wet liver there's a reward," the old man said, struggling to utter the words. His mouth was dry and his lips were cracking. Ahmed wished he would stop trying to speak, since the more he struggled, the more the cracks spread. And the long beard frightened him. The man looked as if he'd never cut his hair in his life. Every child is told the story of the old wise man who was falsely accused and imprisoned in a pit for forty years. Ahmed knew it well, but he never thought he'd meet this hero, the man who defeated injustice and tyranny with endurance and kind words. The sight of the old wise man almost made him forget about Zarga.

"Let Zarga drink as much as she pleases. She is no different than any of my children," the old man said, abandoning the story he was trying to tell and clearly addressing the herder. No one could disobey the old man, not even the herder whose stick had been using him to beat an innocent animal. He spoke with the power of truth and righteousness, and not of tyranny and the violent tools of subjugation. The emphasis on "my children" came as a surprise to Ahmed. The old man had never had children, because he spent all his life in the pit of hell. But as Ahmed turned to look around, the whole drinking herd turned into small children. Zarga looked just like Ahmed when he was very small and wouldn't drink his milk, not because he didn't want it but because he wanted to defy his parents. Ahmed's mother would dismiss his rebelliousness. "Never mind! The neighbor's dog barked at you," she would say, as if he were not the cause of his own actions.

Now Zarga and Ahmed were one and the same. The size of the camels didn't change; they still stood on all fours, with only their faces turned into human faces. Ahmed needed to urinate badly, but he couldn't, no matter how hard he squeezed. As he tried, he lost all his clothes and the strong wind blew them away. He was walking naked through the camp, trying to get back to the tent. He tried to avoid people, but they kept crossing his path and greeting him. He tried to cover himself with his hands. Ashamed, he was wondering how he would survive among the people after they had seen him naked.

Suddenly the wife of the herder with the long stick appeared, with a small child she was ordering around. The child was helping her prepare something, but Ahmed couldn't tell what it was.

"I saw a young camel with the Moroccan herd that matches Ahmed's description of the one that he is missing," said the bearded wise man.

11

MOHAMED WOKE Ahmed by gently tapping him on the tip of his foot. Ahmed had barely slept, and he was more exhausted than ever. He felt drowsy and heavy-headed. He noticed that the lady of the tent was talking to her child as she prepared lunch, a meal he knew the family would do without on any other day.

Ahmed went outside the tent to urinate. In the camp people don't have stinky and disgusting toilets like those he'd seen in the city. Taking care of other business required waiting for nighttime and going beyond the hill, but to urinate one didn't need to go too far, provided one didn't do it too close to the mrah, because although animal urine cures people, human urine makes animals sick. His urine steamed as soon as it touched the hot sand. When he was done, he used a handful of sand to wipe the drops off his body. Like all Bedouins, Ahmed often resorted to sand to clean; it was as good as any water, as far he was concerned.

M'barka had already laid the table, though of course there was no table. Putting the small plate in the middle of the straw mat was an invitation for all to share what little food the family had. No utensils were offered, needed, or wanted, because everyone ate with their hands from the same plate. Like his hosts, Ahmed rarely ate lunch, so the rice with ground watermelon seed was an unaccustomed treat. A thin layer of rice, well cooked and mixed with the seeds, covered the plate to its edges, and miraculously, a few pieces of meat were strewn over the top—a luxury the hosts couldn't possibly have afforded. It was a miracle Ahmed had witnessed many times in his own camp, too, as neighbors quietly honored the custom of helping those on whom the burden of guests falls.

As a child, he used to envy guests when he saw them surrounded with all the good foods his camp had to offer. As a sign of politeness, the guests would send it back after barely touching it. But Ahmed, salivating, was in no mood to return the food. Because his hosts were humble and nonjudgmental, Ahmed was freed from the burden of acting nobly and unnaturally.

The four of them sat around the small plate and devoured everything, in a silent competition to decide who could eat the most in the shortest time. The men picked up the two bones that remained and took them back to where they sat. With one motion, Ahmed shattered his bone against the southern tent pole— avoiding the north as a matter of wisdom, since it is there, or more precisely in the northwest, that the unseen demons and jinn wait to feed on the bones—and sucked out the marrow. A man could do that; a nomadic lady would never do such a thing in front of men, especially one who is young and still looking for a husband. Clean, sharp white teeth are the treasure of any young nomadic lady, and using them on a bone could dull and even break them.

M'barka brought out a copper plate with a silver teapot and three spotless tea glasses. The teapot and plate were handcrafted by local blacksmiths, which meant they were weaker than the ones made in France or in China, but they were prettier, and the taste of tea made with a traditional set is much better. One taste was enough for Ahmed to know whether a set was local, Chinese, or French. Tea from a Chinese set tastes of balsam. Tea from a French set tastes like it was mixed with gasoline.

Most families didn't own expensive sets like this, and those that did reserved them for important guests or for social occasions such as weddings, child name-givings, or big holidays. Perhaps for M'barka a fat meal like this one was extraordinary enough to warrant using the special tea set. In all likelihood, though, M'barka's family couldn't afford such a set at all, and it, too, had been delivered unseen by a neighbor.

M'barka took her time making the tea, clearly savoring the process. When it had boiled to the right concentration, she emptied the glasses back and forth into each other to make the foam rise high, the sign that the mixture of sugar and tea is just right.

Ahmed and the husband were discussing the best course of action for Ahmed to take. They were confident Ahmed would find Zarga in the end, so long as she was alive. But he needed to bring her home: not an easy task. A camel doesn't have four feet, as most laypeople think: it has at least a hundred, and the more the better. A lone camel does not know where to go. Most of the time it wanders crying until it finds its herd, or another herd, or, God forbid, dies of exhaustion. Driving a hundred-camel herd is infinitely easier than driving a single camel. Zarga was a good girl, but driving her home would be a challenge.

The tea was so thick and strong you could almost flip the glass without spilling it. It was just what Ahmed needed to set his head straight after the fat meal he'd been blessed with. As the first cup settled in his brain, he formulated a good idea of where Zarga should and would be. With luck, plus his expertise, he'd catch up to her before she could cross into another country and become subject to a different tribal jurisdiction.

The day had cooled down just enough for Ahmed to venture outside. He gulped his last cup. As much as he would have loved to sit and savor it, he knew that all good things must come to an end. He didn't indulge in superfluous and empty courtesies like thanking the family, the way they do in the cities. It was enough for him to express his gratitude, friendship, and loyalty to this family silently, and when the time came, both parties knew he would deliver what he was called upon to do. Bedouin families don't expect courtesies, but they expect you to be there when you're needed.

Ahmed slowly wrapped his turban tight around his head. A Bedouin's turban serves endless purposes—a pillow, a mat, a blanket, a rope, a dressing for an injury, an indication, in its fabric and color, of who he is and where he comes from—but its essential use is lifesaving protection against the desert's scorching heat by day and pinching cold at night.

"Pray behind me and blow it my way!" Ahmed said as he saddled Laamesh, looking at M'barka, the person he suspected was closest to having her prayers answered. Men are good, but they sin more than women. Women stay close to home and don't have to use a stick or fight over water and grazing grounds, and so don't have as many opportunities or temptations as men do. On top of that, women tend to memorize many more rhyming prayers.

"InshAllah!" M'barka and Mohamed responded, almost in unison. Mohamed evidently assumed Ahmed was talking to him. But nomadic women notice much more than men, and M'barka was paying attention to Ahmed's eyes and saw he meant her.

Mohamed glanced at her and smiled, recognizing his mistake. He watched Ahmed's preparations through the thick cloud of smoke he sucked from his pipe and released without inhaling. Mohamed Junior picked his nose with his right hand and dropped it quickly to help his other hand hold his small boubou around his waist, to keep it from touching the fresh circumcision wound. As if announcing Ahmed's departure, Mohamed's pipe ran out of smoke, but Mohamed kept sucking on it anyway, as though hoping more smoke would come. He squinted at Ahmed. The sun was still intense enough to keep the small goats under the trees, and he was deep in thought, almost like a philosopher.

Ahmed led his camel outside the camp, deep in thought himself, mostly about his positive experience with this good family. Though he had not yet found Zarga, being around good people made his heart joyous and satisfied, and he allowed himself a sense of pride at the quality of friends his instincts had led him to get to know. Had he fallen on negative people instead, even finding his camel would not have prevented him from feeling desolate and sad.

As he was heading out, Mohamed returned to the tent to take refuge from the burning sun. But M'barka grabbed some sand with her right foot, lifted it up, and caught it with her hand. She mumbled a supplication into her hand, blew it into the sand, and threw the sand toward Ahmed. She recited the famous poem to thwart the evil spirits that can ride along and put an extra burden on the camel:

> I'm going out to Allah as his guest,
> truly the guests of Allah will find comfort and face no hardship,
> I'm the guest of the only one,
> O Allah, Guide the travelers on the righteous path!

Every once in a while Ahmed looked back at the tents to gauge his distance, until he could not tell them from the small trees. It's bad luck for a traveler to look back, because it puts doubt in his heart, which makes evil spirits think of him as a weak person. One should never show weakness to the forces of evil; they can smell prey like a German hound. But Ahmed couldn't help it. Good or bad, nomads always remember their encounters, and he knew he would always savor the memory of this meeting.

When the tents disappeared below the horizon, Ahmed made his camel kneel so he could mount it. Laamesh rose as soon as Ahmed's right foot reached the withers, a move that would have sent a bad rider tumbling. For Ahmed, it would have been juvenile to mount a camel this way in front of women and children, but here, alone, he could unselfconsciously let his skill show.

Ahmed briefed Laamesh about his plan for what lay ahead. He asked his camel to be patient and understanding, and started on a hida. Ahmed always sang the same songs when he was alone. His voice was sweet, but it only came to him when he was alone and in good spirits. From time to time the crazy idea came into his mind of being a professional singer, and if it weren't for the dishonor that came with it, he might have pursued this. Only the lower castes were allowed such a career without being frowned upon or shamed. They could find their calling and pride in singing.

The sun set behind the sand dunes and left a hot-colored painting behind. It was a signal to Ahmed to take a break and perform his evening prayers and supplications. His plan was to ride through most of the night, as far as he and Laamesh could. At the third hour before the break of dawn they would rest. If the past was any guide, he would need to sleep for a couple of hours before daybreak.

He dismounted the camel, washed his arms in the sand, and recited his prayers quickly. He could hear how silence sounded. This was no place for human beings; even desert dwellers used it only as transit territory. As he drank from the pure and cool breeze, he felt light and clean from the inside. He mounted again and finished his prayers on the back of his camel. He felt a little guilty about having to ride Laamesh as much as he had, and as much as he would need to do in the coming days. But his guilt was softened by his drunkenness from the perfect breeze and weather, and he was feeling good about his prospects. This wasn't an hour for worry or bad feeling; in fact, it was a perfect time to dismount, sit on a dune, and drink a cup of tea. But alas, he had not thought his quest would take him this far, and so he hadn't brought his traveling tea set.

With Ahmed sitting comfortably in his saddle, Laamesh resumed his pace, slightly faster than a walk but well under a gallop. Ahmed had learned to dance with the camel, following the camel's rocking to protect himself from injuries, especially to his lower back. He didn't need to study physics or medicine to do this; his subconscious did the job for him.

He took out his bait and started to prepare his pipe. One thing Ahmed could always do, no matter when or where, riding, walking, standing, or sitting, was smoke. Smoking could always substitute for food, drink, or good company. With one hand occupied with holding his stick and Laamesh's tether, he used his foot to hold some of the pieces. It was dark now, and he needed to be careful not to lose any part of his smoking kit. Finding a small piece in the soft sand in the darkness of night would be next to impossible. God forbid that Ahmed should find himself unable to blow the smoke up, and his worries with it, to dissipate into the infinite desert sky.

After the smoke comes the singing, and Ahmed started to sing again, running through some of his favorite hidas for his own benefit and that of his companion. Around them, the vast desert was silent and the sky was clear. The bright moon bathed the dunes, and the dunes recycled the moonlight, so Ahmed could see everything as far as the horizon: a rolling ocean of sand with only a few scattered trees to break the monotony. He savored the Sahliya, the fresh breeze from the Atlantic Ocean that is the no-mad's only relief from the hot, dry daylong wind of the Sahel. It brings life back to everyone and everything, starting from the shore and washing slowly eastward over the vast desert, fighting to reach its most remote regions. "The ocean threw up," the lo-cals would say as the wave passed over them.

Ahmed could sense Laamesh's tiredness, and he was in no better shape himself. He worried about sleeping in the open with nothing beneath or over him, especially with his earlier ordeal still fresh and vivid in his mind, but he was so tired he couldn't think clearly. He rode some more, scouting for the best campsite.

He found a hill he judged would be the safest place to camp, with enough trees in the neighboring valleys to entertain Laamesh for the rest of the night. He lightly bound the front legs of the animal with a rope, discouraging him from wandering too far in the merciless desert. He wrapped the tether around the camel's neck and gave him a gentle tap, allowing him to go. He was asleep before he touched the ground.

12

EVERYTHING AHMED had learned in his nomadic upbringing taught him never to run: nomads learn to walk at a moderate speed to save energy. Running is fatal, and life in the desert is a marathon, not a sprint. But in his dream that night he was running as hard as he could, with something pushing him and telling him that this was his only option to survive. To his dreaming mind, his home camp was not that far, and if he didn't reach it before the break of dawn he would die.

To his left, Ahmed saw a large group of people running in a random formation toward the southeast, leaning slightly toward the east. They weren't talking or communicating in any way, just running to safety with all the power and energy they could muster. Bending his direction toward them, he ran and ran as fast as he could, from one hill into a valley and up the next hill, and on and on.

He was trying not to lose sight of the running group. Something inside him told him that he needed to catch up to them and join them because they were headed to safety. Where that might be did not concern him at that moment. Ahmed had learned that priorities are forced by circumstances and not by people, and are often changed by external factors. What he needed now was a level of perfect concentration that would match a Chinese martial arts master. He needed to exclude the fear of the unknown and enjoy the new world around him. Nothing around him was of his choosing, and he needed complete calm and surrender.

Some of the group were lagging behind, and he tried to catch up to the stragglers. His first instinct was to ask them what was going on, and why nobody was allowed to stay in this country. As he got closer he recognized some of the runners. He saw the brother of his cousin Sidi Mohamed, his grandmother, and other people who had died. And yet these running dead didn't look dead at all. They were full of energy, and looked younger, and much healthier and stronger, than when they left this world.

Nothing of the scene unfolding before Ahmed seemed odd to him, not even the fact that the dead looked and acted exactly like the living. He'd sometimes forget that some of the people he was running behind were not alive, and then he'd realize again that he was among the dead. But none of this seemed to have any effect, negative or otherwise, on his mind. There was no difference between the living and the dead or the past and the future. He could clearly remember events that happened in the future as well as those that had happened in the past, with no distinction between them. It was as though the straight line of time that we are running along at all times had bent itself around him in a big circle, with all events equally observable to him in that moment.

The way home seemed extremely difficult and dangerous. He had never been to this place before, and the treacherous mountains weren't familiar to him. The cliffs were very sharp, almost sheer, and looked deep into the valley that lay beneath, some of them more than a hundred ells straight down. The people running with him seemed to have no problem, jumping into the valley and climbing up the next mountain seamlessly. But when he got to the first cliff, he froze.

He looked down to the valley below and saw that it was hard and even ground, with clear trails of wild zebras who had paused along the valley to scratch their backs and bellies on the hard ground. He knew he would never survive the fall, and yet he knew that there was no other way home. He looked right and left and saw nothing but darkness and danger.

Ahmed summoned all the courage he could muster, closed his eyes, and said the last prayer as his grandmother had taught it

to him, the prayer for the departed, over his living body, because
he knew there would be no one to perform it over him.

There is no god but God.
O Allah, forgive and have mercy upon me, excuse me and
pardon me, and make honorable my reception. Expand my
entry, and cleanse me with water, snow, and ice, and purify
me of sin as a white robe is purified of filth. Exchange my
home for a better home, and my family for a better family,
and my spouse for a better spouse. Admit me into the
Garden, protect me from the punishment of the grave and
the torment of the Fire.
O Allah, forgive our living and our dead, those present
and those absent, our young and our old, our males and our
females. O Allah, whom amongst us You keep alive, then let
such a life be upon Islam, and whom amongst us You take
unto Yourself, then let such a death be upon faith. O Allah, do
not deprive us of his reward and do not let us stray after him.
O Allah, I am under Your care and protection so protect
me from the trial of the grave and torment of the Fire.
Indeed You are faithful and truthful. Forgive and have mercy
upon me, surely You are The Oft-Forgiving, The Most-
Merciful.
O Allah, Your servant and the son of Your maidservant
is in need of Your mercy and You are without need of his
punishment. If I am righteous then increase my reward and if
I am wicked then look over my sins.

And then he jumped.
He felt as if he had turned into a small, light feather, with
no control over his speed and direction. He could steer neither
left nor right, nor up or down. In fact, he was floating higher. He
had wanted to get to safety, to catch up with the strange people
he found himself among. But now he was going everywhere but
where he needed to go.
Ahmed kept flying, uncontrollably and ever higher, until he
felt the cold breeze of the moon and the scorching heat of the
stars. When he finally let go and gave up fighting, he felt a huge,

refreshing relief. He was not just accepting but relishing what was happening. He gave himself to a fate of eternal flying.

After a while, without any effort on his part, he landed gently in the valley below, an endless narrow canyon carved by a dried-up stream that looked as if it had battered the valley for seventy thousand years, though maybe the waters themselves were older and had come from another universe to be recycled in ours. On the huge canvas of the canyon walls, nature had painted the most amazing shapes and forms. In all directions he saw the beautiful smiling faces of people and animals, standing in defiance of danger and the elements.

He recognized a natural statue of Zarga's grandmother. She was smiling and looking at him, as if to say *Enjoy yourself*. She looked young and strong, with no sign of the pain she had endured before she died, after she had been bitten by that big evil fly. He searched the other formations, hoping to see the people his grandmother had told him about: a stingy family that wouldn't lend salt to their neighbors and as a punishment when they died were turned into statues made of salt for all to see, a reminder to everyone of the fate awaiting those who turn a blind eye to fellow humans in need. Ahmed was lost in the beauty of the shapes, but he didn't find the salt family.

Though the valley was dark, Ahmed could see that until recently it had been full of life. He made out the most amazing trees, with so many green leaves and thorns that three camels could get full from just one tree, without needing to move. Green grass that smelled of recently fallen rain covered the valley. Birds of all colors were singing and chatting. Traces of camels, snakes, gazelles, and people were everywhere.

Across the valley he saw a steep hill he'd have to climb if he was to have any hope of reaching the ones he loved so much. Climbing up is always easier than climbing down, but he could see he could not do this on his own. Without exception, all the people he'd seen earlier had made it up the hill. On the ridge, the runners were sinking up to their thighs in the sand, but that didn't seem to slow anyone down. How could they be so strong that they could bulldoze through the sand like a devil-twister?

Try as he might, he couldn't attract their attention and get them to help him. He wished they would drag him up, but he knew that just getting them to acknowledge his presence would give him the strength to climb up as they had done. Company alone can give you extra force. The devil was the reason that Ahmed couldn't get over the obstacle, and the devil is a coward: like a wolf, he always looks for a lone sheep to attack and devour. Ahmed shouted and screamed until his voice failed. Then he tried camel sounds that only come from the mouth and don't use the lungs, until his mouth hurt and he could do no more.

How can people be so cruel and self-absorbed? If just one or two of them would slow down and look toward him, they would see him, give him water, help him run, and loosen his tongue to communicate with them. But hoping and wishful thinking weren't going to get Ahmed anywhere. This must be the day of judgment, when all people are only out for themselves, as his grandmother used to describe to him with the most vivid details.

He contemplated spending his remaining days in that dark canyon and living off nature like Hay ibn Yagdahn, the boy who was found and raised by a gazelle. He lived with the animals and ate and drank as they did. He couldn't speak like humans, but he grew up to be strong, beautiful, and instinctive. Because Ahmed had always been good with and to animals, he was sure most of them would accept him as one of their own. He was less sure about the lions and wildcats, but he hoped he could show them that he wasn't a threat, and that he wasn't fat enough to satisfy their hunger.

What he was scared of most of all were the evil and invisible wild animals that he'd spotted with his mind's eye roaming the valley and acting like bosses. He'd never seen their like before: some had three horns, some only one, and they all spoke a language he couldn't understand. If he couldn't leave the valley, it was a question of time before he stood face-to-face with those evil creatures.

In all the great many times Ahmed's heart and mind had been subjected to trials and tribulations, he had never felt sadder or lonelier. He found himself reverting to childhood, completely forgetting the pain in his throat and shouting at the top of his lungs the name of his mother.

"ZAHRA!"

13

HE SHOUTED so loudly and painfully that he woke up scared and shaking, soaked in his own sweat. The place looked eerie and unfamiliar, and he was afraid a ghoul might emerge from any quarter. Anything might be out there, looming, waiting; it was well before sunrise, and the darkness didn't allow him to see far enough even for a safe perimeter. Unconsciously, he started to mumble indistinct prayers. The movement of his lips and tongue helped hydrate his dry mouth, and the prayers and supplications centered him.

Ahmed normally loved to sleep outside the tent, taking his chances with the dew that can make you sick but that he found comforting. He enjoyed the manageable danger that loomed in the dark night. Wild dogs, hyenas, lions, and wildcats could get close enough for him to hear them; he'd feel a little scared, but not truly threatened. Whenever he heard the sniff of a wild animal close by, he would squeeze himself under the thin cover of his boubou and pretend it was his uncompromising mother, wrapped around him to ward off dangers. A feeling of defiance and security would wash over his skinny frame, and he would smile through the turban that covered his face, giving himself to the late night's cold breeze.

As he came back to his mind, he thanked Allah that he was alive and put his hand over his aching, violently beating heart to calm it down. He was more tired than when he'd fallen asleep, as if had been carrying salt bags all night between Chinguetti and Sudan.

For a while he couldn't sit up. The pain that had taken over every bone in his body pinned him to the soft sand that was his bed. He wanted to remain lying there, but not to fall back asleep, fearing the further torments that would take over. A nomad tries to keep spirit and body balanced, but there are two extremes in which he has no control. When he sleeps, his soul flies somewhere else and spirits can take over the body and play with it as they please. When he gets angry, his own mind acts like an evil spirit. His mouth dry, tears flowing out of his eyes and mixing with the sand on his cheeks, he let himself rest a moment. The early morning breeze felt so good: what he would have given to stay like that and let the breeze caress him!

He pried himself from the ground, lifting his upper body and twisting it carefully to spare his aching lower back. If it wasn't for the morning ritual prayer, he wouldn't have bothered to try to rise until the golden morning sun bathed him. But his grandmother had warned him never to skip morning prayer under any circumstances, precisely because it was the most challenging to keep up. Maneuvering to his knees, he struck the clean sand with his open palms and wiped his face with them mechanically. The more he cleaned, the stickier his face became. He tried to recite his prayers and supplications, but found he couldn't remember them. He was best at everything when he didn't think about what he was doing. He started again, thinking nothing. Soon he could hear his grandmother, and joined her in singing:

Bread is distributed between first light and sunrise
It belongs to those who busy themselves with prayers and not
    the unwise
It is written in the old books
Those who sleep in this time deserve no bread
For it's all about the actions and not the appearance
Something that should be obvious to every smart-head

When he was done he sat with his legs folded and his face toward Mecca, thanking God that everything he'd been through was just a bad dream, a way for the devil to make him sad. The passage from sleep to wakefulness is not a quick one; Ahmed knew that he would always have to navigate the buffer zone where he could see both the physical and the spiritual world. But awake now, he remembered that he really had lost Zarga: this was not part of any nightmare.

He was exhausted. His lips were cracking and his throat ached. Even if he had enough saliva, it would be torture to try and swallow it.

Dawn was spreading across the horizon, announcing a new beginning and telling everyone that no matter what happened yesterday, today has nothing to do with it. The sun cleanses the sins of the previous day, every day. But as it reached farther into the desert, the new day's light revealed a telltale mound of human bones nearby. Horrified, Ahmed realized that he had slept beside an isolated grave that had been partly exposed by the battering winds.

How he could have missed it was beyond him. He had been warned time and time again about graves, but his tiredness must have conspired against him. And yet as terrible as the discovery was, there was relief in it as well: now his tormented dreams made sense. He crawled closer to the grave to greet the dweller and read him the usual prayer.

> Peace be upon you all, O inhabitants of the dwelling amongst
>   the believers. Indeed we are, Allah willing, soon to follow.
> We ask Allah for well-being for us and for you.
> Peace be upon you, house of a believer! When my day
>   comes, I will join you as God wills.
> O Allah!
> Forgive the living and the dead!
> Forgive those who are present and those who are absent!

Forgive our men and our women!
Forgive the young and the old!
Give us faith as long as we live and faith as we die!
Honor us with honoring our dead!
Don't lead us astray after their passing!

If the dead man was anything like Ahmed, he would enjoy this fresh blood bringing him the news and the gossip from the camp. But there are certain taboos one should never break. In addressing the man from the other side who was dwelling in that abandoned grave, Ahmed made sure to avoid mentioning the sick people in his clan. The dead can smell their sickness and will seek them out to speed their departure, in order to get some badly needed company. When Ahmed introduced himself, he made sure not to reveal his age, or else the dead man could get jealous and throw a spell on him to get him prematurely killed. Any person educated in matters of nomadic life knows these things. Nor did he pray for a long life, especially over the grave of someone who had surely died tragically, at far too young an age. That would be in bad taste for anyone, even for a French person.

Ahmed now realized how serious his situation was. Had he dreamt that the dead man had carried him away, he would have had to give a camel and a hundred sheep with clean heads in charity, and feed a poor person with camel milk every day for a hundred days. Otherwise he would have died within those hundred days.

Ahmed was humbled: he could see himself in the grave. One day he would be the one being mourned, and he only hoped that he would leave the sweetest of tastes and memories behind. But he knew that even those who loved him, instead of visiting him and enjoying his company, would generally avoid his grave. There would be no blaming them, since they would run the risk of getting hurt by the bad spirits that can live around the graves of even the most revered among us.

He had no doubt in his mind that when his day came, people would say good things about him. He'd heard them saying good things about people everybody knew were bad, and regular people were practically declared saints after their deaths, when the living wove legends around them. No one knew who started those legends, just like no one knew who started the common jokes and words of wisdom. Why did people somehow become better when they died? He wished that, if people were going to say good things, they would say them before the person was dead, when that person could really use them.

Ahmed wondered what scared him most about death. Was it the transition from being totally in control, with his feet firmly on the ground, moving about his business and following his camels as he wished, to his new life beneath the ground, helpless and limited, without even the ability to accompany and sing to his camels? One must adjust when one moves from one grazing ground to the other: was death anything like that? Or was it the ultimate trial that awaited him, the one his grandmother had told him about in the most detailed fashion, where all his sins would be laid out and measured against his good deeds?

14

ACCORDING TO his assessment, there should be a nomadic camp not far from where he stood. He picked up Laamesh, who was still grazing on a tree down the valley on his northwest. It shouldn't be more than a good journey's ride between him and the Moroccan border. What does a border look like? He pictured it as a long, straight line made by the French to separate the grazing grounds and keep the tribes in groups. That way they could control them easily by ensuring either unquestioning loyalty or else war and subjugation, and they could collect taxes more efficiently. He'd never been in this territory before; maybe the border was closer than he thought. Maybe, if it was only visible to local governments and the French, he had already ridden past it.

As he scanned the horizon for tents, he felt a wave of goosebumps washing over his dry body. The place was eerily quiet, with no sign of life, not one single sound. In a nomadic camp, sunset and sunrise are the times when people are loudest and most active, making the camps obvious from great distances at this time of day. But if there was a camp near here, it was as silent as in the midday heat or dead of night.

Ahmed was worried. His instincts were speaking to him, and his instincts were always right. Ahmed could ride for days on end without seeing a breathing soul and it wouldn't bother him. He'd done it before, and he could do it now. The meal he'd eaten yesterday could easily carry him one more long day. The water he had left in the guirbah was good for at least that long, and Laamesh could hold out for another five days. It was not the emptiness as such that had him scared and feeling strange, but what filled the emptiness. It was not being able to spot what he knew was there.

He practically stumbled on the tent before seeing it. How could he have missed it, a man with the senses of a wildcat? It was as though he had been blindfolded and the blindfold had been suddenly removed. As soon as he saw the tent, the strong smell of a nearby mrah hit him. It awoke all the good memories and gave him a feeling of security he badly needed. But it was only a small herd and a lone dark tent, and they made him anxious to leave. This was nothing like the world he was used to.

He'd never seen a tent like this one. Maybe he was already in Morocco, a country he had heard so much about in the stories his mom told him before he went to sleep. The tent was circular, interwoven with tree branches inside the wool, and instead of two poles it hung from a single pole that stood in the middle. He had missed it from afar, mistaking it for an ugly dead tree—camouflage, apparently, to mislead the French tax collectors, the raiding gangs, and even, he realized suddenly, nomads like him. But why? He'd seen all kinds of tricks to avoid the tax collectors and the gangs, which was perfectly legitimate, but he couldn't come up with a logical answer as to why someone shouldn't welcome wandering Bedouins. The heads of all Bedouin children are filled with stories about demon settlements, tales to make one's hair stand on end. Now Ahmed was standing before the very thing he'd been fearing as long as he could remember.

He mumbled the usual prayers for that unusual situation, making sure at the same time not to irritate the demons or to scare off the good spirits. He needed a hot cup of tea, even if it was offered by a family of demons, and he hoped they might even offer him some food, once they understood that he wasn't there to do any harm or try to share the territory that was theirs. He wasn't sure he possessed the kind of power to communicate this, the Secret of the Letter, but he had to take a chance. There were elders in his family who could control and compel demons by reading certain supplications. Such powers run in some families, which made Ahmed a good candidate as well.

Cautiously leaving some extra distance between himself and the tent, Ahmed slowly knelt Laamesh at what seemed to be its front. The camel descended grudgingly, grumbling. A tired camel is a volatile and uncooperative animal, and he could easily have dismissed Laamesh's grunts as a complaint and not a warning. But as Ahmed started to remove the saddle to give his camel some rest, something pinched him hard between his neck and his belly button. He could see how the saddle had started to stick on the camel's fur and dig into his skin, making visible dents: that clearly argued for removing it. Arguing on the other side was the sharp, sudden pain. A nomad's instincts are a communication between his body and the world around him, and Ahmed had survived many perilous encounters by recognizing these communications. He left the saddle on.

If he was really lucky, the tent would belong to a harmless, or even helpful, jinn family, perhaps one that was left behind when its tribe moved to Mars forty thousand years ago and had been wandering ever since. But the surroundings and the setup definitely suggested demons. Armed with his charms and his prayers, he was ready to face whatever the host might be, even if it was one of those demons grandmothers describe to their grandchildren, with eyes arranged vertically instead of horizontally. He rehearsed in his head how he should react in that situation. He must show neither fear nor wonderment. Demons are like us in many ways, and are offended by the same things we are. The main distinction is the extraordinary powers they possess, such as the ability to metamorphose into any form they wish.

He had encountered a demon once, when he was just a little kid. One dark night he was sick and couldn't go to sleep. All he could hear was the snoring of his mother, his father, and the next-door neighbors. Suddenly a pitch-black cat with the brightest, bluest eyes appeared. She looked right at him and told him in a crisp, clear voice, "Ahmed, I need food." He was startled at first, but then remembered that animals can talk too, but choose not to because the universe must be balanced between talking and listening. Realizing that the human race was doing more than its share of talking, the animals decided to listen more and talk only in an extreme emergency. Ahmed broke off a little piece of ground peanuts mixed with sugar that his mother had given to him because he couldn't eat dinner. The cat took it and left as quickly as it had appeared.

In the morning he told his mother about it. To his surprise, she not only believed him but told him that she used to hear small animals talking herself when she was a little girl. A black cat, she told him, meant that the visitor was a demon; the white ones are jinn. The cat came back once, but this time his father was awake and it said nothing; it just acted like a cat. He felt sad because he didn't want to seem like a liar, but his mother told him that metamorphosed spirits talk to us only if we're alone, because they feel safer that way. So many things happen around us, but we can only sense a tiny portion of them, and that portion is reduced even further the more people are around.

But if Ahmed's personal experience with demons was thin, he knew a great deal about them thanks to the legends. Demons are equipped with six fingers instead of five, giving them a stronger grip and more power to crush bones, which are their favorite things to eat. Demons rely on what humans dispose of for their meals, and the most plentiful part of their garbage is bones. They did not like eating them at first, but Ahmed had heard that a seven-hundred-year-old demon from China suggested adding Indian spices, which helped. The demons vowed to keep this secret to themselves, and to punish any spirit who dared to reveal it by hanging him from his hair in the emptiness between the Himalayas and Hindu Kush for eternity. Ahmed didn't know what punishment was reserved for humans who betrayed this secret, but he decided to be on the safe side and never repeated the story to anyone, for fear a single spirit might hear him and report him to the demon tribal chief. Demons remember everything we say and do, and they can use it against us at any time if they believe that we are acting against the interest of their tribe.

Ahmed always got a chill when he remembered the story his grandmother told him about the nomad who spoke ill of the biggest demon tribe. He was just an ordinary Bedouin, with a normal herd of camels, which had been passed down through the generations from the time the Spaniards kicked all the Bedouins out from their Andalusian paradise. He had a fat, beautiful wife and a beloved son. One day, when he and his friends were driving their herds home, he told them that the biggest demon tribes were chasing the smaller ones, taking their lands and sending them to bad places like Nigeria. His friends all thought this was unfair, and cursed the powerful tribe. The Bedouin arrived home and found that his son had been bitten by a vicious snake, which had showed up as if it had fallen from the sky, and disappeared without a trail to follow. Even the strongest-sighted one in the freeg, an old man who'd lost his eyesight and started to see stars in the middle of the day, couldn't see the trail.

The boy died instantly, and the poor loose-tongued Bedouin was submerged in agony and sadness. After days of mourning and prayers for his lost son, he realized that the tragedy happened shortly after he'd told the secret story about the powerful demon tribe. The demons' vengefulness didn't stop there, for the mother was made infertile, whether from the smell of the strong venom or the shock she suffered at seeing her child passing away, the hajjaba couldn't tell. They would never have another child. But in its way that was a blessing, because the descendants of the cursed would be cursed as well.

Stories like this taught Ahmed he was being listened to at all times, and he'd learned to say and do only things that he would not be ashamed of when he was confronted with them.

He shook off the fear that was trying to take hold of his stomach and heart, and a feeling of safety and serenity washed over him when he remembered a poem that he could sing. This beautiful poem never failed him and he'd never forgotten it, because supplications that can be sung stuck in his heart forever. Because they are constantly moving, nomads can't carry around great quantities of books, so they have to rely on memory, and memory's best friend is singing and poetry. Ahmed knew many things by heart, but only if he sang them.

The authenticity of this poem was unquestionable because it rhymed perfectly in Hassaniya, and no good poet could possibly tell a lie that reverberated through the centuries to shame his descendants until judgment day. It was the kind of well-crafted poem the imam of the camp repeated whenever he wanted to prove the veracity of an account or a religious requirement. It had once delivered Ahmed through the darkest of graveyards, when he stumbled and was paralyzed from his waist down and could go no further until he recited it.

The poem read:

> Among the jinn people, I chose the good guys,
> The companions of our messenger, as my bodyguards,
> Sharaf, Monsheen, and Nasheen
> Shasser and Jaber ibn Amer, I have seen
> Nasser, and the seventh of the Seven is
> Ahkab, so leave me alone and go please
> He who knows those names cannot be touched.
> Cannot be touched!
> Cannot be touched!

Ahmed sang the poem in the sweetest voice he could muster, using the rhythmic mode known as Makamat. Though "Makamat" was a word he'd never learned, he knew what it was by feel, and exactly how it went from one line to the next. He repeated the last sentence seven times, as people did, though the repetition was not actually part of the poem, to make sure any invisible person who was listening got the message. He blew lightly onto his chest through the boubou's opening at his neck. Then he rubbed his hands against each other and wiped his face and the top of his head with his palms, in the natural area of his hair, though it had long ago receded. He slid his hands to the back of his neck and rubbed them several times back and forth, making sure no ill would be allowed to hit him from behind when he wasn't paying attention or was in a vulnerable situation such as sleeping or being distracted by preparing a fresh smoke. After the ritual he felt strong and untouchable.

15

AHMED HAD hardly stepped away from Laamesh and turned toward the tent when a very tall and extraordinarily fat woman emerged. If it weren't for her old veil and the lack of facial hair, he would have greeted her as the man of the tent. Her face was wrinkled, with strong jaws and a long pointing nose. There was a hint of former beauty to the nose, but this woman looked nothing like the kinds of delicate women Ahmed grew up around. Her hands were big and rough, likely from doing men's work.

"Salam alaikum!" she said impatiently in a deep, hoarse voice, not waiting on her guest, who was supposed to start by declaring his peaceful intentions. She extended her big rough hand to greet him. The veins of her well-defined arm popped out like the roots of an old desert tree exposed by persistent winds and dune migration. He was taken aback, but he kept his composure, and counted her fingers in a quick scan to confirm what he was expecting to see. But the strange woman had only five fingers.

This hardly eased his confusion. The family might be mixed, he reasoned. He'd heard of such things before, from an old man who'd read it in a rare book written by an Iraqi man during the Abbasid dynasty. The old man said one of the emirs back then declared intermarriage between humans and jinn and demons lawful, though only under strict conditions. In those days, people wanted to try anything new because so many different people with different customs had gathered in Baghdad, and they had tried just about everything. Like most of us, Ahmed thought that things are good if people around you do them but bad if no one does them, or if only people outside your tribe do them. But once we find ourselves amid those who live according to other customs, we start to understand and even appreciate them.

For instance, when he was a child and his mother took him to the city for his circumcision, they stopped at a boutique and asked for a drink because they were thirsty. The owner was happy and received them just as a nomad would under his tent, but he made them pay for the drink. Ahmed was shocked, but later he saw that all the store owner's neighbors had their doors closed, and the owner could not go to them to eat and drink tea. He had to buy his own food. In return, he sold drinks to people to pay for his food. It was weird, but everyone agreed on it, and life went on like in the camp, but with less generosity—or maybe it was just a kind of generosity that required reciprocity.

The more people saw and tried, the more they burned to see and try more. And as for intermarriage between humans and demons or jinn, the French hadn't bothered to regulate that at all, but of course that was only because they were simply too blind to see the obvious.

Sometimes Ahmed, modest man that he was, was amazed at how much he knew about the unseen world. By listening to the accounts of the elders, he had accumulated all the knowledge a nomad needs and more. To encourage him to listen and learn, his mother used to tell him, "Learning as a child is like carving on stones." In fact, old people are just as able as children to learn this way, but time is stretched for them, so that one day for a child is equal to seven for grownups, who can go whole days without ever once listening and who too often convince themselves that they are unworthy or unable to learn new skills.

And though Ahmed had never stood face-to-face with the unseen world like this, he had sensed its presence on many occasions. He felt it most often after sunset, when he was walking alone in the dark. He would feel a chill running down his spine, and looking around himself for the reason, he often found that he was near a graveyard, a trash dump, or an animal that had been killed rather than dying on its own. But now he found himself facing the very demons he'd heard about so many times. Hearing about the devil is nothing like standing before him, and here Ahmed was, with a demon standing tall, in flesh and blood, right in front of him. No matter how much you think you are prepared for such a moment, Ahmed could have told you that you aren't: nothing his grandmother had taught him over the years to fight off evil spirits came to his mind. He stood there with an empty memory and a body that was about to be delivered to the mercy of a merciless demon creature.

The eyes of the woman were big indeed, and yet the opening between the lids was horizontal, not vertical as he expected. So much for his theory that he was in the tent of a demonic family. He was relieved, but also disappointed. A part of him had wanted to go through the experience of being with demons; it would be a story to tell his children, even his grandchildren. Provided, of course, that he lived to tell it. It is such stories that create legends around renowned families, legends that they live and breathe the way regular human beings breathe air. But of course it is much easier and cozier to hear these legends around tea and a fire, surrounded by those one trusts and loves, than to be the story itself.

A human she was, but the closest a human being could get to being a demon. She was freakishly strong, imposing, and had dark and sparkling eyes, sharp eyes that nevertheless betrayed that she was hiding something. They were the kind of eyes that could see a caravan from a forty-day distance and the track of an ant in the nighttime in the total absence of the moon. No one needed to tell Ahmed that: he could see that she had freshly applied Arab mascara with its secret ability to sharpen eyesight. In her mouth were the remnants of freshly chewed schtooka, the powerful Moroccan tobacco that was so popular in the region. Despite—or perhaps because of—this habit, her teeth looked both ugly and surprisingly strong.

But who was this woman who had shaken his hand? The only people Ahmed knew who dared to shake hands with the opposite sex were the French or those who had been around the French for a long time, like his cousin, the translator Sidi Mohamed. Unless he is a member of the family, a man always greets a woman only by talking, not by touching. When the nomads first met the French, they considered these greetings in extremely bad taste, even a sort of sexual harassment, until the French explained to them that greeting everyone this way was part of their culture and no one was offended, even French women who lived in big castles.

The woman smiled dishonestly at Ahmed, revealing even more ugly teeth. He could easily recognize the line of the Sahel, as it's called by the locals, the thin brown line running along the top of the upper teeth that builds up from the minerals they drink in that region. "Come on in! What do they call you?" She spoke quickly and impatiently, with almost no emotion. Her dialect was unfamiliar, but he could understand it, more or less. And though her manners were rough, Ahmed knew well that one often has to lower one's standards regarding religion and customs, and in strange places like this only the bare minimum of decency could be expected.

Ahmed felt sad and lonely in this foreign territory. He must have crossed the border without noticing. So this is Morocco, he thought. His grandfather had recounted so many stories about the sheikhs, Marrakesh, and Ibn Battuta, who had traveled the whole world and seen where the sun hid during nighttime, and the Sea of Gihoon, whence the sun rises every day, and the land of Sheikh Ahmed, who made the journey to Mecca in one night, flying on his prayer rug and smelling the Egyptian spices of Cairo as he flew by. He had even told Ahmed that half of their tribe was still in Morocco, and while Ahmed's half had safeguarded the traditions of their ancestors, these distant cousins had lost their ways to the French and the Germans. Morocco, once the country of alchemists who could turn stones into pure gold!

But Ahmed was not in this country to turn stones into gold. Even if he could, it would be a big responsibility to divide up the gold and give zakat to the needy. He would be happy if he could just find his camel and bring her back home.

"Ahmed Ould Abdallahi from the tribe of Idamoor," Ahmed replied. "Am I in the kingdom of Fez, with the sea full of jewelry, and Marrakesh, the city of the king who owns a thousand thousand pieces of gold?" he asked hesitantly, deliberately shifting the attention away from himself and toward a general subject.

She ignored his question and scanned him up and down. "Herder, eh? Looking for a stray camel? My husband's coming soon."

She probably just didn't understand his question. Kingdoms meant little to people this deep in the desert, Ahmed reflected. To them a small and vaguely defined water source and its territory belong to a tribe, but tribes are allowed to wander back and forth, in a tacit understanding that they can use another tribe's grazing grounds and water as they did their own. This had been true for many centuries, except when a war erupted between two tribes. When that happened, it could sometimes take many generations for the wound to heal and the animals of the one tribe to be allowed into the territory of the other.

Most wars start when revenge is sought after a homicide. If the offending tribe does not provide justice by turning over the perpetrator or asking for forgiveness and offering camels for the grieving family, tradition and honor require the victimized tribe to seek revenge by killing a random person of equal value from the other tribe. The more blood is spilled, the longer the cycle of violence lasts and the greater it grows. Ahmed knew to follow the tribe when it called for revenge and never to ask why, because that would be a sign of cowardice and disloyalty. As a child, he had memorized a poem that says:

> They'd never ask one of their own,
> When he calls upon them in his fight

In time of need, distress, or when he's down
For proof that he was right.

Everyone knows that this long tradition of revenge was started when Kulaib from the tribe of Taghlib killed a she-camel belonging to his wife's aunt, a woman by the name of Bassous who was from the tribe of Bakr. Bassous, seeing the horrible act, cried out and called for revenge. Bassous's nephew Jassas answered the call and killed the perpetrator, thus avenging the camel. And so a bloody war of revenge and counter-revenge was launched between Taghlib and Bakr that would last for forty years. Ahmed's feelings about that war were divided. True, one must pay for killing an innocent camel. But innocent people must not be made to pay for what others have done.

Ahmed was uneasy. Why should this odd-looking woman start a conversation when it was obvious she was not interested and couldn't carry it out? She certainly hadn't made a good first impression. But efficient people, which she clearly was, don't like to waste their time in small talk and exchanging niceties: this was a woman with a plan, a very evil plan.

16

AS AHMED entered the tent, the stench of rotten meat hit him, making his eyes water. It was an odd smell; they must have animals in Morocco that weren't in his country. It was odd, too, that there was meat at all, since the family looked very poor. The braided palm and leather h'sairah was so beat up it was like sitting directly on hard sand. But who knows? Ahmed thought. Maybe in Morocco meat is very cheap.

The smell seemed to be coming from an arahhal, the wood-framed, carpet-covered saddle that carries women on camels and converts to a storage rack inside the tent. It was bigger than the ones he was used to back home, and packed full of stuff he couldn't make out, because it was carefully covered with a cannabis-rice bag. A dirty tea set, also bigger than the ones he was used to, lay on the ground on the edge of the dirty mat. The pot was painted, but too caked with sand to make out the color, and the two glasses were too filthy to see through.

Someone must have died here recently, Ahmed thought. There was a darkness and macabre serenity inside, and he was reminded of when his great-uncle passed away. The colors of his grandmother's tent were fainter, and the sun wasn't as bright as on other days. Her tent smelled funny, but from what he couldn't say. That smell, which he later learned was the smell of death, was here. He felt for the first time what it might feel like to be inside a grave.

The meanness of this old lady must have been caused by the loss of someone dear to her, he thought. Such a loss is painful, but even more so if it is coupled with guilt toward that person. That this woman was guilt-stricken seemed clear, though Ahmed had no idea why; she had guilt written all over her face, and there was a silent cry for help in the corners of her hard eyes. Guilt devours the soul, as fire devours dry grass in the desert. Perhaps she hadn't tended to the person when the person was sick. When Ahmed's great-uncle fell sick, Ahmed did not tell his mother about a prominent hajjab who was living in a freeg a half a day away, for fear she would send him to summon her. And when the old man died, Ahmed wished he had walked seven days to save his life, but alas, it was too late. Things that matter matter most when they are gone. Or maybe the death here had been a violent one. The blood that runs through living things is dangerous, and when blood is spilled and cannot be buried with the body, it leaves its mark on everyone.

Ahmed sat half-heartedly on the edge of the mat, barely touching it, ready to change positions or move on if he was asked, or ordered, or felt he should. He felt torn between the need to get some rest and a cup of tea—if luck was still on his side, he might be offered some food as well—and his need to feel safe and at ease, which he most certainly did not. The result was a stalemate that left him perched on the edge of the uncomfortable h'sairah. He thought of the expression about the mat containing the fiber that is foreign to it.

The muscular lady-man of the house poured a half-cup of thick, rough tea into the dirty cup and drank it in one big, loud gulp. He was shocked; it was traditional to taste the round, but, out of respect for the other tea drinkers in attendance, one was supposed to do it with a tiny sip.

She filled both cups and, without saying a word, handed him the cup she'd just used. He could still see the oily marks her thick lips had left on the teacup. Ahmed never shied away from sharing cups and bowls; that was what everybody did and should always do. He had seen a long mustache submerged in the bowl of zrig, and he still drank out of it, and he had eaten with men who picked their noses before sticking their hands in the shared plate. But now, for the first time, it gave him a queasy feeling, made worse by the woman's habit of sticking her tongue in and out in a quick, uncontrollable motion.

Apprehensively yet hungrily, torn between need and fear, Ahmed took the first sip, avoiding the marks left by her lips. She kept a close watch on him with the side of her eyes, never saying a word. He did the same, stealing a glance whenever he thought she had stopped looking at him. Every time, he met her stationary and unblinking eyes. He had never in his life felt this uncomfortable in someone else's tent.

The tea was as thick and bitter as a Moroccan harira at the end of a cold Ramadan day. He forced himself to swallow the bitterness like a French medicine, for he needed some green tea in his system for the long and lonely journey ahead. He'd drunk sugarless tea before, when his grandfather had run out of sugar, and brewed tea by itself has its own sweet taste. Maybe she had just brewed it way too long.

Ahmed remembered the time his father's father ran out of sugar. He threw away the tin where he kept it. Ahmed was surprised; one never throws away things that can't be replaced. The tin was a gift from his uncle to his grandmother, bought on one of his trips to Senegal. It had held candies, square bite-sized caramels that melted in your mouth and stuck in your teeth so you could savor them all day.

Ahmed asked his grandfather why he threw away the tin. "Leave it to Allah! He will fill it with sugar and give it back to me," said the old man with a confident smile and the air of an extremely devout man. That same afternoon a small commerce caravan passed by the camp, and everyone was able to exchange gum arabic and local fruits for sugar, tea, and rice. This had never happened before: the main and only caravan always came in the first month of spring, when the jinni of poetry comes back from hibernation.

From that day on, Ahmed was convinced that no one was greater than his grandfather, who could cause miracles to happen.

Suddenly Ahmed felt funny. His lips thickened and grew as heavy and numb as two big bricks hanging from his mouth. His tongue stretched and filled his mouth. He tried to lift his left hand to touch his mouth, but he had no sense of touch, and his hand weighed so much he couldn't control it anymore. Everything was moving in fuzzy colors, with small, bright dots.

The cup of tea in his right hand became heavier and heavier. Ahmed fought to take another sip, but he couldn't lift the cup in his shaking hand. This was the definition of a nightmare for him. In his bad dreams, he would be tortured by not being able to eat the good food he saw before him. Now he was holding a small cup in his hand filled with the drink he needed, and yet lifting the cup to his mouth had become as impossible, as they say, as forcing a cat onto its back.

Even a patient nomad like Ahmed, who had been trained to deal with his emotions privately, could grow frustrated, even angry, if pushed far enough. He tried to drop the cup, though that would mean committing the sin of wasting sweet food. He thought of his grandmother, who would pick up fallen grains of rice as her way to thank Allah and show appreciation for His provision. "Just think about it, Ahmed! If someone gives you a gift, you should take good care of it and use it for the purpose it was made for," she would tell him.

But his hand wouldn't release the cup. He tried to shake it loose, but nothing happened. His hand stayed frozen in place, like the wind-sculpted figures he had seen in the Valley of Salt, sculpted by jinn artists to impress their kings and make human kings jealous. To the jinn, human kings are petty, childish, needy, and power hungry, unlike their own kings, who consider themselves slaves of their people.

Ahmed knew he was falling victim to a bewitched cup of tea. But did his host know it, too? For all his fears about this woman, he refused to believe she could be responsible for such an atrocious act. He searched her face for any remnants of humanity. He tried to call out and seek her help, but he couldn't talk, blink, or wave. He sat looking at his unmoving and silent host, as if staring into his own image in a funny mirror.

One, two, three, and he was gone. He disappeared into a blackness so complete it held his dreams until the day he died, when all that had been hidden to him during his life was revealed to him.

17

AHMED WOKE up heavy and tired. He did not want to wake up, and had no feeling for place or time. He tried to sit, but couldn't. He wiggled himself back and forth, trying to change sides, but he couldn't summon the necessary force. His quest to bring back Zarga was gone from his memory. He knew only that he was Ahmed, a proud nomad. As he struggled one more time to shift his body to the other side, he realized that his hands were tied to his feet. Why?

At first he didn't necessarily see this as sinister. Maybe he had gone crazy and these people meant to protect him from himself. He had never known how it felt to be crazy, but at that moment he might have enjoyed discovering that feeling, if only to prove his theory. But if this was how it felt, it was like having the load of a big camel divided evenly over your body, like having the tongue of a cow shoved into your mouth and a bunch of big sharp needles inside your stomach. It made the easiest of tasks feel like going to China on foot, in summer, and without a camel. Being crazy wasn't a good feeling after all, he decided.

The lady of the house sat a few feet away, staring at him. She took some schtooka from a bundle at the end of her veil and some ash from the dying fire beside her and mixed them well. She then took a between-two-fingers portion of the fine tobacco powder, squeezed it so hard it was as if she wanted to make it disappear, and quickly and hungrily snuffed it, pushing her nose open with her thumb to get all of the tobacco inside. Ahmed's eyes teared up from the strong smell, but she didn't even sneeze.

The lady then started rearranging the arahhal, moving pieces of meat still on the bone from one side to the other so they would dry the right way. Dried meat can be kept for many months, even years, and can be eaten in many ways. As it is, without cooking, which was the way Ahmed preferred. Or beaten slightly, with hot hump fat added to make it softer. Or added to cooked rice, crumbled and sprinkled over the dish in many tasty recipes. Ahmed's eyes hung heavily, but the strangeness of the meat gave him a jolt and kept him teetering between sleep and wakefulness. He could see it was from a big animal, but he couldn't tell what. It must have been bigger than a goat but smaller than a good calf, and much smaller than a grown camel. A small camel would have had longer bones, and a small calf would have had thicker bones. Maybe it was one of the Moroccan wonders his granduncle would read about in the book with flimsy yellow pages. And the meat was nothing like the meat of a camel, cow, or goat. It was particularly red and stinky, the stench so strong it pierced his nose and pried him, at last, from his drugged sleep.

A muscular man wearing only a pair of baggy, dirty black nomad trousers sat outside the tent. The smell of his pants was contaminating even the smell of the meat. He was sharpening a big knife with a tiny dull file. As strong as he was, the effort was futile, like trying to convince a Yemeni to change his opinion by force.

The man was sucking energetically on a bone pipe, made from what looked like the foreleg of a goat, but even larger. It still had specks of meat on it, perhaps the same kind that hung from the hammock. He was a big man, but the pipe barely fit in his mouth, forcing the smoke he exhaled to pass through two tiny windows at the corners. What Ahmed wouldn't have given for just one drag from his own pipe, to distract himself from the world around him and bring him back into the much friendlier world inside his head. But he had resigned himself to doing nothing for now, not even smoking. A silent voice was telling him that to get back his freedom of movement he would have to wait until the opportune moment.

The man wore distinctive charms: a small metallic square around his neck and two small leather balls on his upper arms held in place by his bulging biceps. On his big left toe he wore a copper ring that made a clear dark indentation, and on his right ear a small gold earring. Judging from the look of the man, the guy who had sold him the charms was no fake: this was one of the most robust nomads Ahmed had ever seen, outside of his tribe at least.

The woman of the tent was berating the husband as she arranged the meat on the arahhal. To a thousand sharp words from her, the man would offer one. From the way they spoke to each other, Ahmed could tell that she was the one who wore the pants in the tent. He couldn't understand the language they were speaking. He knew Arabic and Zenaga, and he'd heard and partially understood French, Wolof, Fulani, Soninke, and Bambara. But this dialect was like nothing he'd ever heard in his life. And yet what people say doesn't matter as much as the way they say it: no language can express your friendliness and happiness better than an honest smile; conversely, a frown and a disrespectful look are all you need to express the pain you're carrying inside. As the Bedouin song says,

> Your eyes told my eyes about the secret you meant to hide,
> Your heart hides the resentment that your eyes truly show.
> My mouth remains shut because of my pride,
> But my eyes can always tell who's my friend and who's my foe.

This woman was not happy. She was speaking from one side of her mouth, while the other side was filled with so much tobacco it looked like a balloon. Every few words she would spit straight in front of her, without giving the man the courtesy of looking away as she spat. She seemed full of saliva, because she was spraying even as she argued. Probably she was cursing.

Ahmed felt no more pain, but he was so tired, and every bone in his body was crying for a sip of water. His throat was sore from dehydration, and he was desperately trying to gather his own saliva and swallow it. His tongue had shrunk from a big balloon into a dry piece of meat.

He was in the center of the scene without being a part of it. No one addressed or acknowledged him; it was as if he were an invisible ghost or a hidden observer. While the woman was berating her man, at the same time she was taking care of him, handing him a hot cup of tea, for instance. Ahmed realized he wasn't crazy after all. To crazy people, tea smells like milk, which is why they try to drink it in one gulp and burn their mouths. But to Ahmed the tea smelled like tea. But if he wasn't crazy, he had to conclude that his hosts must be.

As his head slowly cleared, he was flooded with questions.

Why did they drug him?

Why did they shackle him like a crazy bull?

What else did they do to him while he was unconscious?

How long had he been unconscious? Hours? Days? It couldn't be months, because his fingernails were still short . . . or could it be?

Ahmed had learned from his father that every question is legitimate, and every question has an answer. His father taught him this when, as a teenager, he had struggled for days to ask about the embarrassing changes his body was undergoing. But life also teaches that those who have the answers to our questions often withhold them. And so Ahmed had also learned to trust his ability to find his own answers when those who ought to provide them chose silence instead. This ability had saved him from many dangerous situations. It didn't matter if his answers were not correct at first; as time went by, his answers would become better and better, light would shine over his soul, and everything that was hidden would reveal itself. Secrets are like a stray camel that has joined your herd. Sooner or later the light of day will shine upon it and it will be recognized for what it is.

The logical answer that came to his mind was that he'd just been captured and would be sold into slavery in a faraway country, a practice he'd heard was common in his grandfather's time, when bandits attacked peaceful families and kidnapped people for profit. If that was the case, he knew he wouldn't be sold to people that looked like him, because humans everywhere are ashamed to enslave those they consider their own kind. They would take him to a place where his speech and look were different, and sell him to people who would let themselves be blinded by these differences and trick themselves into believing he wasn't fully human. Being different, ironically, would give him the power to endure beatings and abuse without it hurting as much. He wouldn't feel ashamed in front of his abusers, because they wouldn't be able to see him for what he really was. He would be wearing a sort of invisible cloak that concealed him from them.

But if his master was friendly enough to share food with him instead of abusing him, if he respected him and gave him chores he could perform and allowed him to sleep when the sun went down, it would be a different story. He wouldn't be able to steal food for himself. He'd feel visible, and would need to be careful not to dishonor his tribe and family. Slaves understand honor, too, often better than their masters. So it was with Bilal, who chose faith and dignity and endured many days of torture on burning sand at the hand of his master, until the meat peeled off his back. Bilal's faith and dignity turned his master into the slave of his own tyrannical self, and the slave in bondage into a master in his own mind, and in the minds of people for generations to come.

As a child, Ahmed had heard stories about these raiding tribes. They took animals and goods without paying for them and sold the humans they stole as slaves, even when there was no war. They were a fearsome, unpredictable hand that descended randomly to collect a cruel tax from the nomadic and peace-loving tribes.

When the French colonized the country, they cracked down on the practice and made it clear that taxes could and would only be paid to the new master of the land. Though the practice of slavery lingered, in the end the French won, because they had guns and cars and they remembered everything by writing it down. To most nomads there was hardly a difference. Instead of being compelled to pay protection money and ransoms to the raiding tribes, they were being compelled to pay comparable amounts in taxes to the French. And it didn't take them long to see that the French could be brutal masters, too, killing innocent people for simple dissent, or for not doing their bidding, regardless of their own laws.

Yes, the French were strong. But Sidi Mohamed, the interpreter, had told Ahmed what an old French officer told him, that the Germans were even stronger. The officer knew this, Sidi Mohamed said, because he had spent time in a German prison camp during the Great War. The Frenchman was drunk, and warned Sidi Mohamed he should not repeat this to anyone. The Germans, he said, were like the Tatars who invaded Baghdad, pillaging and killing everyone, even children. Like everyone in the freeg, Ahmed knew the story of the Tatars from the *Thousand and One Nights,* and for years after Sidi Mohamed told that story, Ahmed would confuse Germans and Tatars.

In reality, Ahmed reflected in his chains, everyone wanted money: the raiding tribes who stole animals and people; the free French, who could say awful things to their tribal leaders; and of course the family that was holding him. Ahmed closed his eyes and scanned the future. Open eyes distract the mind's eyes, busying them with things that block the line of sight; the future is only visible when one's eyes are closed.

Ahmed figured that he could negotiate his way out of slavery. His clan would offer the family the same amount they planned to sell him for, saving them the cost of carrying him to a faraway place and feeding him for months. To the Bedouin, the clan is a health insurance policy, a life insurance policy, and an insurance policy for practically everything else as well. You can always count on your clan to repair any damage you might cause to others, or that you suffered because of others.

This was not a one-way arrangement. Ahmed had been called upon more than once to contribute to save some cousins of his. A few years before he'd had to sell ten camels and pay blood money to save a cousin who was involved in a fight that resulted in the death of a young man from another clan of the same tribe. At first the family of the deceased didn't want to take the money; instead, the brother of the deceased wanted to kill the perpetrator or one of his relatives, with no particular preference as to which one, except the younger, stronger, and smarter the victim, the better. The rules of nomadic life can be as harsh as the environment itself. But the elders and imams from both camps intervened, and after long conversations, with many invocations of old stories of bravery, forgiveness, and generosity that no one but the oldest in the camp remembered, the settlement was reached.

God forbid, Ahmed thought. What would I do if my family asked me to avenge a murder? So far he had only to pay with his camels. Deep down he believed that killing innocent people was wrong. He never shared this belief with anyone, for fear he would be stigmatized, called a coward, or even singled out to perform some similar tribal responsibility to prove his uncompromising loyalty. Yes, he understood that an innocent man who was murdered needs to be avenged, but how can that terrible wrong be righted by killing another person who had nothing to do with the crime? This question lived without answer in Ahmed's head, next to Why do so many people think that they are better than camels? and very many others.

His senses continued to sharpen, to the point where he could hear the footsteps of a long queue of ants, led by the smell, rushing toward the fatty meat on the hammock and carrying tiny pieces back to the big hole in the sand that was the door to their colony. Like a nomad, the ant doesn't own anything; everything is for everyone and no one. If humans worked like ants, Ahmed's grandmother told him, drank tea, and ate baobab every day, they would live a thousand years without sickness, and only pass away out of boredom.

Ahmed could hear the ants talking and joking as they carried the provisions home, piece by piece. The big ant that remained inside the hole knew exactly how much meat and fat was needed and how many ants were needed for how many trips to carry it. At first, she had sent all the young ants. After a thousand and seventeen trips, she told half of them, the males, to stay at home because the males are stronger but have shorter breath. After another thirty-seven trips, she asked half of the half to take a break. This process had been going on for one and a half days, and would go on until the whole colony had been fed, with the number of ants sent out diminishing until a single ant went back to collect the tiny piece of fat from the husband's dirty pinky, which would feed the last one hundred and eleven of her friends.

The husband, who did not seem to feel the sun that had been cooking his head and turning his neck dark red, did not notice the ants. He kept running his index finger over the blade of his knife to test its sharpness. Each time he was not satisfied and would sharpen it some more. All his senses, faculties, and forces seemed to be deployed to reach the end of a perfect cutting blade. But in order to see clearly and judge a task correctly, one has to step away from it sometimes. Ahmed had learned that wisdom when one day when he was obsessing about a newborn camel that couldn't walk. He had done the right thing, tapping on its hind legs lightly with his stick and singing. But the baby wouldn't move. Ahmed grew terrified that the baby was so sick it would never walk. In the midst of his worry, he was called to an emergency: his neighbor had fainted and needed cat's milk sprayed up her nose to bring her back. Saving his neighbor's life made him forget about the baby camel for a while, and when he came back the baby was walking just fine. He realized that his own anxiety had scared the baby and made its legs heavier, because fear can settle in the legs.

As the big woman rose to go outside and join her man, she twisted her big foot and tripped on the tea set. She fell like an old camel, bringing the arahhal with her as she tried to catch it on her way down.

The meat she had been cutting and arranging was strewn everywhere, and a human head, still intact, fell off the arahhal and rolled over the mat all the way to where Ahmed was lying. It was the head of a young man. His eyes were wide open, and running down his cheeks were two trails that his tears had made. They met at the end of his chin, making a beautiful necklace with his eyes and his eyebrows. His mouth was open, showing his perfect teeth. He seemed to want to say something, but couldn't.

Ahmed's hands and feet tingled, then numbed, and then sent a current of numbness through the rest of his body. He shouted so loudly his voice almost tore a hole in the middle of the tent. He wanted to cry, but his eyes were burning dry and his throat was parched and hurting. He tried to talk, but his tongue turned into a stone. He tried to move, but his body felt glued to the ground.

A bitter taste filled his mouth. His stomach cramped, in an agony worse than anything he'd ever imagined. So many emotions overwhelmed him that he laughed and cried at the same time, but the laughter made no noise, and the tears were so hot they had to run back into his head so they would not burn his dry, warm cheeks.

In the middle of nowhere, minutes before his own passing, with no family or friends to share the pain with him, he allowed himself to mourn himself. He would be mourning when every valley had dried up the rainwater, as they say in the East. Ahmed had never imagined that he would know of his own death beforehand. Like the rest of his family, he refused to visit the French doctors, who insisted on telling their patients about their impending dooms. Why should a nomad ruin what's left of life by being consumed with the knowledge that only months or even days were left to live? A nomad wanted to enjoy life, to work and do good deeds until the very last moment. Why should you spend a month on a painful goodbye when you could wait until the very last moment?

But here it was, that very last moment. These were not slave traders. As a child, Ahmed had heard about desert tribes that kidnapped fat young people and killed them for meat. They would send the meat in caravans to faraway countries, selling it for gold and Asian tiger genitals, which could be used in powerful magic potions to break up families and force men and women to fall in love with people they didn't even like.

From those stories, Ahmed had learned cannibals cannot live without human meat, because their souls are evil and can only survive on innocent blood. They couldn't help themselves even if they wanted to. The more they sin by eating the forbidden food, the sicker they get and the more meat they want. When their children are born, they grind the meat and mix it with milk. The babies naturally throw it up, but after many tries they get used to it like the adults. Wise men outside those tribes said they could break the evil by letting the babies drink the milk without the meat. But cannibals knew that to do that would be to endanger their entire culture.

How painful would this be? Ahmed thought about every stupid argument he'd had with his family and friends, wishing every single one hadn't happened. Or that, because arguments will always happen, he hadn't said what he said when he was angry. He wished he hadn't joined in gossip, or paid attention to the gossiping of others. He wished he had been nicer, gentler, more generous. His grandmother had told him that what he really owned was what he gave away. At that moment he finally understood what she meant. Everything he had given away was safe in the hands of those to whom he'd given it, and everything he had kept would belong to the first person who took it. He thought about all the things he would change in his life if he could get back to his life and family. He wished he had been a better man, and that he could have the chance to become a better man. Alas, when it's time to go, wishing is no use.

At that moment nothing really mattered except the few good things he'd done for others. All traces of hate and resentment toward others were erased from his heart. Even toward those who were about to butcher him he had no hate. He only felt bad for them, for the burden of wrongdoing they would carry all their lives and beyond: sooner or later they would find themselves face-to-face with death and bitter regret. His love toward his own family grew and intensified immeasurably. There was nothing he wouldn't have given to kiss them a last goodbye. He smiled broadly and wholeheartedly and prayed to God not to dishonor his family.

What's next? he wondered silently.

He closed his eyes to travel somewhere else, somewhere there would be no evil family surrounded by the meat and bones of dead people. Was there any medium in the whole wide universe through which he could communicate his ordeal to his family? Divided burden is a feather, Ahmed's grandmother had taught him; pain and grief can be mitigated if they can be shared and divided among the people who care about you. Pain is like a heavy tent falling on your head: the more people standing nearby, the lighter the impact. But Ahmed had to bear his burden all alone. As he squeezed his eyes tighter, trying to smother the tears that finally came, like summer rain in the desert, he saw the blinding and soothing light of the moon from a couple of nights before.

O moon!
Source of light in the darkest of nights,
Provider of safety for night travelers,
Give me comfort and show me light.
You sing the praise of Allah in all majesty and silence,

You yourself pray and read supplications.
Between myself and hazard, I put a high fence.
Even the wisest among us cannot read your lips,
But now my inner eye can see as clearly as the rising sun in
    the east,
I can feel you with my fingertips.
Tell my wife and my kid that I love them,
Tell my mother and my father that I love them,
Tell the universe I love it,
Tell Sidi Mohamed to ask the French doctor to forgive me,
As a child, I thought that his perfume stank.
My family shouldn't worry about me,
I'll be waiting for them in heaven until they join me after a
    very long life.
I'll be waiting and tending their house.

Ahmed had never uttered so strong a poem as this. He said it in a kind of trance, and when he woke up, it was being sung in a loop in his head.

Ahmed was confident that his family had received his message, and most of all his mother, because she had stopped sinning at a very early age, and so Allah had cleared her mind like a mirror and given her the unlearnable knowledge. Many times, when he returned from a trip, she had told him about the difficulties he'd encountered. When he asked her how she knew these things, she told him that she had felt a cramping pain between her heart and her belly, in the place where he had lived for nine months.

18

THE POEM and devotional prayer had revived him. He could feel his feet now, move his hands, and pray and sing with his tongue. The last was what he needed most, for the tongue is the most powerful weapon, even more powerful than a sword. A sword can kill only one man at a time, but a word can kill a hundred; a tripping foot the doctor can heal, as the Bedouins say, but a tripping tongue can lead to the grave. His only chance of surviving and going back to his family now would be to defeat the fear that was gripping him. His grandmother had told him that fear is the biggest ally of the enemy, because the enemy can send it to you to disable you, without having to do anything else but watch you unravel.

He decided to engage his captors and negotiate with them, if only to buy time. "My tribe is very rich. If you release me, they will give you a hundred pregnant and fat she-camels, more than anything you can get for my lean meat." For the first time since the encounter began, the husband looked at him with something resembling human eyes. Ahmed could even see in them, with a great effort of imagination, a flimsy respect.

The man kept chewing at his pipe as though he wanted to crush and eat it after smoking.

"I need a drag. Haven't had one forever," Ahmed said. To suggest this was to risk the man's wrath, but if a man allows you to take a drag from his pipe, putting your mouth where his was, it creates a bond between you. The thought disgusted Ahmed, but a smoke is a smoke. The beast seemed taken aback, as if suddenly uncertain who was in charge. He handed Ahmed his pipe. Aside from the saliva contaminated with human flesh and fat, the tobacco was first class, and it sent Ahmed into a trance, where he felt untouchable and robust.

"I don't think there's anything your tribe could offer us that would nearly match the pure Asian gold we'll get for your meat." The man spoke slowly, and to Ahmed's surprise he could understand the local dialect well. Speaking clearly suggested a kind of respect, a willingness to communicate. "Our clients buy just about everything, you wouldn't believe!" the man continued, smiling slightly. It did not seem to occur to him how horrible the thought that seemed to amuse him would be to Ahmed, or to any other feeling human being.

The lady was watching the conversation carefully, but she seemed to be in no mood to be part of it or start one of her own, even if she had been able to spit out a couple of sentences that anyone could understand. She certainly didn't seem like one who would be interested in doing favors or indulging in negotiations. If the milk isn't bad, don't spill it and hope for better milk, as they say. But as she looked with slight disapproval at Ahmed and her husband, it was clear she condoned this negotiation, at least for the time being. This was the kind of breakthrough Ahmed had been looking for. Maybe he could drill through the concrete wall and establish a solid line of communication.

Ahmed continued trying to persuade the man to take his offer. The man was much more understanding than his wife, and seemed to be as much a victim of the woman as Ahmed was of the couple. He was bad, no question about that, but some evils are less evil than others. If he had been born in Ahmed's tribe, he might have been an honest herder, too, but here he was, so madly in love with this woman that there was nothing he wouldn't do to please her.

Ahmed's grandmother had taught him that Satan never asks someone to do bad things all at once. He always invites his prey to follow him, offering baby steps toward the real goal, knowing that when the target agrees to follow, he will eventually commit the sin. Ahmed found himself trying to imagine the path that brought this man to this life; it was as if sharing the man's pipe had opened his eyes, too. He pictured a young, handsome man crossing paths with a family and falling in love with their mysterious daughter, not knowing this family was the last remnant of some terrible cannibal tribe. He could see him marrying her against the will of his parents, and being shunned by his own family and tribe. Bit by bit his wife would have introduced him to cannibalism, starting him on dry meat she claimed came from rare, exotic animals. He loved it so much he asked her for more, and then more, until it was an addiction. In order to fire his passion, she would keep it from him, giving very little at a time. "I made a mistake and gave you the wrong meat," she finally told him one day. "I'm sorry it was human." Then she kissed him tenderly. The man, by then, was long gone.

The man and his wife conferred in their strange language. They seemed to be arguing the merits of his proposal. Ahmed followed the conversation with his eyes and ears, paying special attention to the tone and gestures. The man seemed to be leaning toward compromise, if only to do a favor to a man who shared a pipe with him. But his wife appeared unmoved, as if afraid to do good lest she discover and nurture within herself an inner goodness that would defeat the evil she needed to eat human flesh, suck the blood, and crush the bones.

The evil woman won. Ahmed wasn't surprised; his grandmother had told him that people with the weakest argument always speak the loudest and intimidate the most. The conversation over, in a quick motion she grabbed her innocent prey by the neck of his boubou, which clung to his skin with a thick black layer of accumulated dust and sweat. Ahmed's weak and battered body was no match for her. He had seen how muscular her arms were, but he could not have guessed just how freakishly strong she was. As she pulled, she tore the boubou, exposing his neck to allow her husband to cut through it. To make it easier to maneuver him, the woman cut the rope that was binding his feet to his hands, knowing as long as she had him in her grip he could not flee. For some strange reason, she seemed to want his face directed toward kiblah, probably more out of habit than any desire to allow him to look toward the holy house that Abraham had built for his children and receive a last blessing.

Ahmed raced to recite Shahada: there is no god but God and Mohamed is God's messenger. His supplications were rushed, his shaking lips barely touching, as if he wanted to hasten a response. He was switching between the Shahada and the crisis prayer, "Ya Hayyu, Ya Qayyum!"

> O Living!
> O self-sustaining Sustainer!
> I take refuge in Your mercy,
> Lead my actions and deeds and bless them!
> Do not leave me to my own devices, not for the blink of an
> eye, or less than that!
> O God! O God!

The husband hesitated. "Well?" his wife shouted. He had sharpened the knife to ensure this moment would be quick, but now, for one critical second, he wavered. She twisted Ahmed's head violently, snapping the string that held the hajab his mother had given him when he was little. Ahmed strained to hold the charm to his neck with his chin. The husband pointed to it, mouth open, frozen. His wife seized the charm and flipped it to him. He looked at it for a second and squeezed it tight in his hand. His eyes turned red and his temples wrinkled and beaded with sweat.

"Scheiße!" It was the worst curse word Ahmed knew. He'd learned it from his cousin, who learned it from the drunk French officer, and hearing it again made Ahmed queasy. Where had this man learned it? If uttering a French word meant even a good person's prayer would go unanswered for forty days, what evil would come from a cannibal uttering a German curse word? "Who gave you this shit?" the man screamed, shaking with anger and fear.

Ahmed could barely understand the words the man was struggling so hard to utter. "Serigne Ibrahima," he stammered, taken aback by this change of direction and nervously offering the name of the sheikh whose power infused the charm. Why should the man care where the charm came from?

"Don't you lie to me, or I'll ki—!" He caught himself, realizing that threatening to kill him wouldn't be effective under the circumstances. He moved closer, pointing at Ahmed's face. "What's wrong with your finger?" The man suddenly had a thousand questions about his strange guest—none more pressing than how he'd come to possess a powerful original charm from Sheikh Serigne Ibrahima, who had died years ago, and who had defied the French on more than one occasion.

Ahmed had completely forgotten about the wild card hanging around his neck. Sometimes the best solution is the simplest and closest one; it's easiest to get dehydrated when you're close to water, as the Bedouins say. He had forgotten how far Sheikh Ibrahim was known and how widely he was respected. He was feared, and more importantly loved, in many countries along the Sahel region. Good people loved him and bad people hated him, but those who hated him would never dare to say it openly, for fear his powerful tazabbout might strike them.

"My finger was bitten by a possessed snake," Ahmed answered. "As you can see, I had to cut it off." Ahmed saw a real glimpse of hope. A division was developing in the enemy, and he needed to use it cleverly. The man had clearly had enough. The smart thing is always to leave a little breathing space between the person you are pushing and the corner; for the husband, the corner was having to risk his life, and worse, risk losing his soul by opposing a charm as powerful as the one Ahmed was wearing.

The man faced his wife and gave her a good piece of his mind. Ahmed missed most of what the man said, but his body language conveyed the message better than any words. "Hajab . . . Sheikh Serigne Ibrahima, son of Sheikh Serigne Mamadou Ibrahima . . . evil desert snake . . . bad news!" *"I'm not stupid!"* he ended angrily. He pressed the tip of the sharp knife to his own temple, not wanting to be disrespectful and push his luck by pointing the deadly weapon at her. Glaring at Ahmed, he spat. He spoke slowly, to make sure he would understand. "May his belongings get inherited!" he said, invoking the traditional wish that Ahmed might be struck dead.

The woman was salivating, her tongue moving quickly like a dog's, and with an exasperated shriek, she dove for Ahmed's neck. The prospect of biting into fresh meat was blinding her to the disaster that would befall if she messed with such a great patron as Sheikh Ibrahima. It was clear to Ahmed the woman did not know what she was up against. She was too ignorant or too isolated in her upbringing to have heard of sheikhs from other countries; ignorant and isolated people have no common sense. Never exposed to the awesome effects of African charms, they can't be bothered to imagine their dangers. Ahmed felt a gentle warmth as the woman bit down. He knew the pain would come much later, when his blood was cold.

The husband lunged for the wife, dropping the knife and the charm to free his shaking hands. The wife dove for the falling knife. The husband fearfully followed the charm with his eyes, too worried about its devastating powers to reach for it. In that moment, Ahmed saw his chance. He caught the falling charm and, holding it by the broken string, slammed it against the woman's exposed leg. The charm's sharp metal edge cut the middle of her upper thigh. An electric shock ran up her leg and paralyzed her entire body for a split second. She was in fact a very lucky woman; if the charm had touched her just one millimeter higher, she would have been paralyzed for life. But that split second was all Ahmed needed to slip past her, scoop up the knife to prevent them from recovering it, and race out of the tent. He had no thought of stopping to use the knife. His mother had told him repeatedly that all sins but one can be repaired somehow; the only exception is murder.

The husband seemed amazed at first, and then enraged. "You'll go free only through my mercy!" he screamed after Ahmed. Knocking his dazed wife out of the way, he took off in pursuit.

19

AHMED NEEDED to find his friend Laamesh as soon as possible, jump on, and ride wherever the camel found it easiest to run. His instinct had told him there was something fishy about this tent, and so he had chosen not to unsaddle his camel. In fact, if it had been up to Laamesh, Ahmed would never have entered the tent in the first place.

As soon as he felt there was a small distance between him and the tent, he glanced back. He saw the woman, still stunned, follow her husband out of the tent but veer off in the wrong direction. But when he turned again, the woman had fully recovered, overtaken her man, and was closing in on Ahmed. He could hear her heavy, controlled breathing across the shrinking distance.

As a child, Ahmed would push himself forward faster by opening his mouth wide and raising his head to allow the wind to flow in through his mouth and out his ears. The wind is part of the universal harmony, and when something disturbs its natural speed it pushes back, determined to restore the harmony. To the wind, humans are neither good nor bad, but simply obstacles that have been blown into its path by the twisting storms of their own lives. When Ahmed showed it the respect of allowing a harmonious current, the wind welcomed him.

Ahmed and the woman spotted the camel at the same time, and she redirected her course there. It came down to a simple head-to-head race, with Laamesh as the finish line. The woman kept gaining on Ahmed; his days of torture, desperation, and hunger were starting to pay off for her. No amount of determination and streaming sweat could leave the woman behind.

As they reached the camel, Ahmed saw there was no time to undo the rope he had wrapped around Laamesh's legs, and so he sliced it with the stolen knife. The man's hours of sharpening the knife for Ahmed's neck had come to his rescue instead. The exhausted nomad felt the warmth of the woman's heavy breathing on his bare shoulder blades. He clenched his back and gave her a mean elbow to the chin, throwing her back. As she struggled to regain her balance and charge him again, he jumped up and reached for the front tongue of his saddle, threw himself onto the tall camel, pulled the tongue between his legs, and skillfully twisted his lean body into place. It was the kind of move young men would try to impress the girls of the camp. It hurt a lot more when Ahmed did it now. But pain was something he could worry about later.

Laamesh had smelled his master the second he left the tent: Ahmed's smell, mixed with fear. If only he had two hands like Ahmed's, he would have prepared himself. A bull camel would have charged and destroyed his master's assailants. But a castrated camel can't get angry, and Laamesh did what he did best. He waited. But as soon as he felt Ahmed safely in the seat, he took off like the offspring of an ostrich.

But the woman wasn't about to give up, especially after she had managed to get her teeth into him once. The salty taste of his skinny neck had a flavor she had never experienced. She dove like a hungry cat and grabbed the camel's tail, then planted her feet in the clean sand. Like Ahmed, she had singlehandedly taken down many a camel. Few others in his camp could overwhelm a camel this way, catching its tail and hanging on until the exhausted animal gave in. For Ahmed, with his strength, agility, and experience, it was a quick process most of the time. He would lure the targeted animal with the rest of his herd toward a water point or bowl of salt, then dart in from the side and grab the tail, avoiding the sudden kick that can kill a man instantly and taking care not to harm the camel. He would dig his heels into the sand and not let go, no matter how hard the animal kicked or screamed and how far it dragged him over the rough terrain. The smoother the ground, the more resistance a tailing man can produce by digging his feet into the thick sand, and so the quicker the camel wears down. When the camel loses steam and is too tired to fight, the herder can throw it gently on its side.

Ahmed did not enjoy doing this to his camels. He only did it when it was necessary to get a camel to take medication or be transported or branded. When young, inexperienced herders ignored the cardinal rule of never underestimating a camel's strength, and broke an arm or a leg trying to tail an untamed animal, he didn't enjoy that either. Ahmed never mocked or laughed at them, because when you mock someone, the thing that befell them will befall you, too, before your death. But when the young show-offs managed to escape injury, shook themselves off, and stood up laughing sheepishly themselves, Ahmed couldn't help laughing, too.

The fine sand here was in the woman's favor, but the slope was not. The scene was surreal, and beautiful, too, in a macabre way. The strong young camel was galloping at its top speed, driven by fear and with the wind at his back. Balanced atop Laamesh, Ahmed was yelling at the top of his lungs to chase away his fear and worries. And the cannibal woman was sand-skiing, using the animal's tail and hind legs to stabilize herself, sliding from side to side and playing for time. The breeze and the rushing adrenaline were replenishing her strength, and the camel's first burst of energy was fading.

Ahmed could see the game was not in his favor. He swung his stick and gave her the first blow across her ugly face. She yelled in pain, but only squeezed the tail tighter. "I love it. That's all you've got? Give me more of it!" she cried. Before the pain could die down, he delivered another blow. He didn't want to beat up a woman. He just wanted her to let go and let him depart in peace. As he kept swinging the stick, the woman started to predict Ahmed's moves, synchronizing her switches from side to side to avoid the blows.

Laamesh stopped suddenly, and the woman smacked into the back of his leg with her forehead and fell to the ground. Ahmed would have been thrown, but he had read the animal correctly and held tight to the back of the saddle, raising his stick high to balance himself. Free of the woman, Laamesh could finally catch his breath and resume a regular pace. When Ahmed let himself look back, he could see the woman lying still, all but covered by sand, and, far in the distance, the tiny speck of her husband running to revive her.

Ahmed prostrated himself, thanked Allah, and kissed the camel's back. "May Allah give you a long and blessed life!" he whispered into the camel's ear, pulling his head close with the tether. Ahmed was fresh, reborn, but he knew he would need to put a whole day between himself and people-eaters before he could let himself feel happy. Though it was midday, he pushed on, looking back from time to time for any sign of the cannibals. All he saw was a big sea, a fata morgana, dancing on the dunes.

The reflections on the sand made the baking sun feel even hotter. Suddenly Ahmed was hungry. He remembered many times his family had cooked meat by burying it beneath the sand and leaving it for several hours to simmer. The meat melted in the mouth and tasted like nothing else. But when he actually started to taste the meat in his mouth, he recognized his problem was worse than hunger: dehydration and exhaustion were playing tricks with his senses and dulling his nomad's sense of orientation. He was no longer sure of the direction of his quest. Riding under the sun meant a slow and painful death, as the skin starts to burn and die one cell at a time. The search for Zarga would have to wait: both the man and his animal needed to rest.

But he also needed to keep moving. He had not had time to refill his guirbah, and if he did not find people and water very soon, he might as well have surrendered to the cannibal family. He tightened his turban around his head to seal his mouth, and even tried smoking a couple of times to trick his brain into thinking he'd been drinking water, but nothing could stop the quick process of dehydration. He decided to head south, knowing that was his only chance of encountering another breathing soul. He and Laamesh would rest under the next tree they came upon that offered enough shade for his head and the upper half of his camel. From now on they shared everything: either they both survived, or they both went with dignity and honor.

When they finally reached a suitable acacia, Ahmed knelt Laamesh and tethered him to the tree. He tried not to think about his predicament. He lay down on the shade-cooled sand, using his stick and the end of his turban as a pillow and the rest of the turban to cover his head. He allowed his eyes to close and his head to dream of salvation.

He should have been happy to be alive. How much greater were the challenges his forefathers had overcome! Any time the young Ahmed had complained about his situation, his father would remind him of how easy life had become for the younger generation. Ahmed knew this was true, and he was always grateful for that. And yet he couldn't help wondering whether his grandfather had told his father similar stories, of an even harder life. His great-grandfather must have had stories of his own to tell. And so on. If this logic was sound, he must be living in heaven, compared to what his distant forefathers must have suffered. Or maybe old people always tell such stories to children to strengthen and encourage them.

But Ahmed would rather have doubted his own reasoning than doubt his father's accounts. He tried to calm his spirit by daydreaming about the kind of heaven he needed now, an oasis where he and his camel would drink and eat. Focusing on that good picture, he fell asleep.

20

WHEN HE woke up, the day had begun to cool down. He wasn't as hungry, but he was terribly thirsty. There was only enough water in his guirbah to sustain him for another day. They would need to ride through the evening and night; he couldn't afford to lose even an extra drop of water through sweat.

The water he had left would be shared with Laamesh. If the camel was saved, there was a chance he might be saved, but if the camel went down, he had no chance. He pried himself from the cooling, comfortable sand bed and stood up with difficulty. He felt dizzy and weak. Struggling to open his heavy eyes, he saw the horizon turning a pale orange. Laamesh was nearby, browsing the branches of the acacia. Ahmed leaned into him and ran his hand up the camel's neck.

Camels dribble a lot of water when they drink, so he opened Laamesh's mouth wide, held his tongue to one side, and directed precious drops from the guirbah down the animal's throat, and then a few more drops onto his own cracked tongue. He was even thirstier now, but his eyes opened wider. He untethered Laamesh. As they set off, in his mind he was moving away in a perfectly straight line, but with his head tied as it was, he couldn't be sure. Tied head, as the Bedouins call disorientation, is the ultimate enemy when the most important skill is being able to find your way in the vast, same-looking desert.

Ahmed had not yet had time to deal with his ordeal, or to get sick. At first he was in shock, which gave him the fuel to ride most of the day. Now it was hunger and thirst: when starvation and dehydration threaten, it's very hard to think about the painful past. Your whole focus is on surviving.

Every step was a struggle, as one foot sank and stuck and the other tried to free it before it stuck too. But the late afternoon breeze was cool. As night fell, he chose a small and beautiful dune that hadn't seen a breathing soul in a very long time. He sat on it, facing what he thought to be the kiblah, though he couldn't be sure because the eye of the sun was painted red. He tried to locate the evening star, the herders' star, as people in his area called it, but his eyes were playing a game on him that made him see the star everywhere. Ahmed loved that star. It starts in the west, when it is sure that the sun will not burn it. But it is so afraid of her that every night it runs eastward, away from the sun, all night, only to confront her again at the break of dawn. She gobbles it up and tries to swallow it, but it tickles and hurts her throat, until she spits it out so violently the star lands back in the west. There it passes out and sleeps all day. Then, forgetting everything, it wakes in the evening and repeats the same journey all over again.

He felt the warmth of sand beneath the cooling upper layer. His afternoon rest had given him peace and serenity in spirit, but it had made him weaker. It took almost all his energy to perform the ritual motions, energy his body would not have later. But this was a trade-off that he could accept: given the painful choice between body and soul, he would always pick the soul.

He lightly tapped the sand and rubbed it on his face. His mouth couldn't say the prayer, but he ran it through his head silently. With difficulty, he climbed the saddle, then closed his eyes, giving the reins to Laamesh. A camel can find water better than a man can; it can smell it from a three-day ride away, while a nomad can only smell it a half-day ride away. And Laamesh's instincts were sounder. He would never go back to the dangerous territory where his master had been hurt, and his navigation skills were precise.

The Sahel's breeze was cool and soothing; one could almost drink it. Instead, when the last hour of the day announced itself, Ahmed stopped and forced himself to squeeze a palmful of dark urine, pressing his fingers together so as not to allow any to leak out. He drank the urine in little sips. As a child he had tasted his urine, preparing himself like all nomads for just this moment. It was warm and salty, a little like the French soda he once drank by mistake, confusing it with his medicine syrup when he visited the city with his mother. The urine was so terrible it made him throw up, but he was told that when he really needed it, it would taste okay. Hardly: he still gagged, but he managed to catch the upsurge and swallow it again.

He closed his eyes and drank everything, and then licked his hand. It was awful, and too little even to soothe his burning throat, let alone quench his thirst. But he was satisfied in a different way. He was not the first nomad to find himself facing death and having to fight for his life; for this very situation, there are steps to be taken, the same steps his forefathers and their cousins had been taking for hundreds of years. Ahmed was in the belly of the beast: he was the story itself, the very story he had recounted a million times, when he would feel sad for those who had not taken the necessary precautions, or who were just plain unlucky, and had fallen victim to the desert.

A man can drink his urine three times, after which the urine will kill him. Then he faces the choice of dying or killing his animal, opening its stomach, and squeezing water out of it. Ahmed had heard that in harsher times desert nomads would muzzle their camels to keep the water inside their stomachs, since camels lose a lot of water when they chew cud. He could never do that. Even so, there would be enough in his camel's stomach to quench his thirst, but he would lose his ride and friend for good.

Ahmed threw himself face down on the sand, which had been cooled by the evening breeze. The dew was starting to descend, and there was a gracious ocean breeze. He gathered the top of the sand between three fingers and tried to suck the moisture from it. But the sand stuck in his dry throat and choked him, so he had to spit it out, costing himself valuable saliva. But soon the dew began to sprinkle him, and he was a baby and the dew was his mother gently putting him to sleep.

21

THE MORNING sun did not ease itself onto the scene. It rose impatiently and all at once. Ahmed woke to its scorching heat branding his neck. He tried to stand, but his lower back was aching and his legs couldn't carry him. He was confused and disoriented, and for a moment thought the sun had risen in the north. He thought he heard people's voices around him, but as his consciousness crept back they disappeared. But Laamesh was still standing nearby, though Ahmed had not tethered or shackled him for the night. The camel would not let his friend down.

Laamesh was chewing his cud more deliberately than usual, a slow-motion, hypnotic rhythm that made Ahmed dizzy to watch. There wasn't enough water inside the animal to let it chew at the usual rate. Animals think correctly inside their heads, without expressing their thoughts in a language that we humans understand. The camel knew he had to use the little that was left of his resources sparingly. If it had been up to Laamesh, he would have found his way by now to where he needed to be, but he was ready to die in pain and dignity to try to save his master. It wouldn't be the first or the last time a camel made this sacrifice.

Ahmed crawled toward the camel like the weak and vulnerable baby he'd become. He tried to climb onto the saddle, failed, and tried again. Each try left him weaker and farther from his goal. At last the camel lay on one side, allowing Ahmed to hug the saddle with his arms and legs. As soon as he settled, Laamesh tilted his head slightly and stood up gently.

Ahmed did not have the strength to guide the camel to any particular destination, nor did he try. He abandoned his plan to ride at night: he needed to get somewhere and get there fast. His pain had dulled, and now he enjoyed the sight of the unreal water shimmering through the fata morgana. Hoping for something is better than total desperation.

They rode on. Sometimes Ahmed would laugh hysterically and feel so strong he wanted to jump off the camel and run to the source of the nonexistent water. All that held him back was the voice of his late grandmother, telling him to stick to his camel. Other times he would cry, but without tears. He swung between those extremes until he was exhausted, and only then did he come back to his true self: a man on the verge of dying, whose story might never be told to his children, an end that is worse than death itself.

High up on the camel's back, with the movement of the animal, there was a slight breeze to counter the heat, enough for Ahmed to press on. But soon he could no longer hold himself steady on his saddle, and as much as he wanted to continue, he knew a fall from that height would break bones. He signaled with his heart to Laamesh to kneel down, and the animal obliged. He climbed down slowly, and started to walk on the tip of his toes, drawing in the sand as he stumbled forward.

When there was no strength left in him to walk any farther, he decided to lie down under the next tree. It wouldn't be long, he told himself. He'd get some rest, then carry on. Deep down he knew there was no walking left in him, but he couldn't let that thought take over his mind. A man can only live if there is hope, and death is the cessation of hope. Ahmed's grandmother had told him that with goodness, hope, and faith, one could live a thousand years.

Then he saw it: a clear stream that had been left by a recent heavy rain. He couldn't say for sure how far away it was, but this was no mirage. Mirages change distance and pattern and spread over a much larger area. Here he could clearly see the steady, flowing channel, and the smells of fresh water and dead fish on the banks filled his nose, just as they had when he visited the city of Rosso as a child. He vividly remembered the scene: when he saw the fishing boats dancing on the Senegal River he couldn't contain his joy, and he laughed so hard he couldn't breathe, laughed until he fell down from the pain in his stomach.

A rush of strength and determination flavored with new hope propelled him forward. He let go of all restraint and walked quickly and straight, held back now only by Laamesh, who lingered behind. He should have wondered why his camel failed to smell the water. As he approached the water, he kept convincing himself that it was getting closer and closer. But it wasn't; it would disappear and appear again somewhere else, always farther away. He closed and opened his eyes to make sure the devil of the heat wasn't playing tricks on them. But it was: the demon was actually building fake water to give fake hope to anyone who decided to follow his steps.

This unfunny game went on for some time. Ahmed wasn't giving in to the demon. Go with the liar until the doorstep of the house, as his mother used to say. He would not go that far; that would be impractical. But if there was water, it would save his life; he wasn't going to stop until he knew for sure it wasn't there.

But the devil and his cohorts live and breathe the bits and pieces of pain and suffering that we humans let them have. When the promise of cool water had vanished, stream by fake stream, the rush of energy dissipated, and he felt even weaker and more exhausted than before. He couldn't walk anymore. Ahmed let out a painful cry he couldn't hold in. He decided to lie down and wait for the raging sun above him or the baking sand beneath to take him, whichever overwhelmed him first. He still wanted to live, but did not have the power. He prayed he would lose consciousness as soon as possible.

And yet he was still walking. Lost in a haze where perception and reality were one and the same, Ahmed dragged his feet through the burning sand. He saw the sun now as a big tent providing him shade and shelter. He didn't want it to go down or the day to cool, because that would weaken the sun, his sole protector.

Ahead, on the slope of the next dune, he saw the freshly stripped cadaver of a nomad who had been claimed by the desert. The vultures were busy devouring what was left of his rotten meat and exposing his bones. Ahmed felt nothing, except envy of the big birds for enjoying such a feast. He was succumbing to the days of exhaustion and starvation. His moral compass was failing.

The stench of rotten human flesh was strong. He sat for a while in the sun enjoying it. It reminded him, ironically, of life. Even more ironically, he realized, he had found himself in this place thanks to his ordeal with the people-eaters, and now he was contemplating joining the vultures to save his own life by doing the deed of evil people. There was no way he was going to do that, he told himself. But he could sit there for a couple of hours until he had satisfied himself with the good stench and taken some energy from it to drive him toward the path of salvation.

As he sat there, the vultures, picking up his own smell of death, began to attack him as well. He fended them off, but it was a matter of time before they had their way with him. One enthusiastic young bird snapped off the better part of his right ear. When Ahmed tasted his own salty, nutritious blood running down his cheek, he knew it would mean his undoing if he didn't act fast.

But when he acted, it was as though he, too, had become a vulture. He pushed two of the birds aside, took a bite from the left thigh of the dead man, and swallowed it without chewing. The meat was dry and tasted like goat jerky, but thicker, fatter, and richer. Even that small piece in his empty stomach made a difference. He took two more quick bites before guilt struck. For a second the guilt battled against the urge to save his life, but by the third bite it got the upper hand. He had to move now, to leave that place before he started to enjoy what he shouldn't. He realized the truth of the saying his grandmother had taught him:

He who mocks a sinner will not die before committing the same sin.

Though the dry meat had made him thirstier, it allowed his body to stand straight. An additional force propelled him forward: the need to get away as far as he could from the body and what he had done. With Laamesh too tired to ride, he walked for hours, the tether tied around his waist. He grew weaker with every step. He contemplated going back to the cadaver to finish what he'd started, but it was too far away and he was too weak and the hungry vultures would have picked the bones clean by then. One more time, Ahmed asked God for forgiveness of his trespasses and resigned himself to his fate. He prayed that he'd lose consciousness and find himself in the beyond, in a better place, with no more pain or suffering.

He didn't pass out. He saw a big old tree just a few feet in front of him and crawled toward it, and when the shade hit him he felt the breeze of salvation blowing his way. That's it, he whispered to himself. He thought for a moment of killing Laamesh. But the thought made him nauseous, especially since the camel had already saved his life once.

"Allah will save the both of us," he mumbled as he looked at the unsuspecting animal chewing innocently beside the tree. Animals deal with danger much better than humans. Humans are tormented by remembering past suffering and imagining future pain and death. Animals feel pain and suffering only as they are happening, and spend their lives undisturbed by thoughts of the past or the future. In a way, Ahmed was already experiencing death, but Laamesh would experience death only once.

Ahmed had spoken of salvation. But there was no sign of any salvation. It was a prayer more than an assertion. His grandmother had told him that assertions and positive affirmations were the strongest of prayers. Ahmed didn't want to be awake when death decided to arrive at his doorstep. He only wanted to sleep deeply and more deeply until he passed away. He lay down and put his worn-out turban on his face. In the blink of an eye, everything is gone and nothing matters except for the good deeds and gestures one has done for one's family and fellow human beings, he reflected. "This is it!" he sighed, speaking to no one.

22

HE SAW his grandfather Salem. Salem had died when Ahmed was a very small child, but here he was, exactly as Ahmed remembered him, except that he was very clean and dressed in the most beautiful clothes Ahmed had ever seen. He wore a light-blue boubou sewn with Sarakole motifs, and a milk-white turban wrapped around his head. Colorful feathers were sticking out of the turban, and the boubou was tied around his waist with a leather belt. His beard was neatly trimmed, as always. He held his smooth wooden cane with the hand grip and rubber foot.

As Salem stood before his grandson, he began to grow thicker, taller, uglier, and scarier, until he had ballooned to the size of the fattest man on earth. Yet it was still him, the untalkative man always drowning in his own thoughts, smiling when people made unfunny jokes and looking on disapprovingly when people laughed at the funny ones. He said little to anyone, and dismissed most of what he heard with a shrug or a wry smile. He loved his grandson and shared stories and food with him that he wouldn't share with anyone else. But he would open up to Ahmed only if there was no one else around. He didn't want people to disrespect him and take him for a weak man who couldn't control his own emotions.

I swear to Allah that everybody will die, especially old people, the African saying goes. Ahmed knew that, but he felt especially safe around his grandfather, and was showered with sadness when he died. For some reason, maybe his age, or maybe his grandfather's example, as much as he tried he couldn't cry. But his mother cried enough for the both of them.

That his grandfather had been a holy man was no secret, even beyond the camp. He could make accurate predictions about the future, and sometimes met with the departed and passed messages back and forth between them and their living relatives. These powers were masked by his quietness and perpetual forgetfulness; he had the habit of asking Ahmed his name every day, and sometimes more than once a day. Add to that the fact that he often spoke to invisible people, and it might have been easy to dismiss him as a fool. But everyone had witnessed or heard stories about his gifts. When he spoke to no one he was addressing both the spirits and the dead, Ahmed knew. Ahmed couldn't see them because they wore costumes whose colors were too bright or too dark for him to see.

Ahmed's favorite story was always the one about his grandfather and the miracle of the tea. It was a dire thing when a household's tea supply ran dry: it meant a family's situation was desperate, and it was having the hardest of luck. But on the day his grandfather's jar went empty, a woman from another camp appeared at his tent with tea and sugar, asking for a prayer. She had traveled a long distance in a hurry. She had seen her own grandfather in a dream, and he had told her that he was in a bad need of a cup of tea. She went to a dream interpreter, who told her that she should look for the nearest holy man and give him enough tea and sugar to make tea. The holy man would be her grandfather's surrogate: when he tasted the tea, her grandfather would be satisfied. She asked around and was told that Sheikh Salem was the most righteous man in that part of the country, and so ran directly to him.

Ahmed couldn't remember whether he'd witnessed this story or whether someone had recounted it in his presence. He could remember so many places he had been and so many things he had witnessed, but he could never tell the difference between his childhood experiences and his dreams. He did remember clearly that his grandfather was a man who received many gifts from people seeking to get closer to God.

As much as Ahmed loved him, he could never quite forgive him for one incident. Both the grandson and the grandfather loved sheep's milk. The old man used to add sugar to it and drink it while it was fresh, leaving a couple of sips for the small boy. But this one time Ahmed's father brought the old man his milk, and as he drank it the boy was salivating in anticipation of his share. Closely, carefully, he watched the tilt of the milk bucket and listened as the sounds of the sips grew louder as the amount of milk diminished. The bottom of the bucket kept rising and rising. Sensing the milk disappearing and fearing his grandfather's failing eyesight might be to blame, Ahmed did his best to make his presence felt, but the old man was losing his hearing, too. Finally Ahmed heard a loud sip that signaled the old man was trying to suck out something that wasn't there. The aromatic smell of the milk in the fire-cured bucket added to the boy's pain. Knowing he would never get his share of the milk made his heart ache so much his eyes teared up. Though he could never hate his grandfather, he always remembered that moment as a kind of betrayal, a reneging on a silent contract between the two.

But now Sheikh Salem had come to him. He carried an old skin guirbah, the kind that gives the water a sweet taste and keeps it cold in the heat. He hurried toward his dying grandson with steady steps and a look of worry on his face that Ahmed had never seen before. The closer he drew, the louder his footsteps got and the larger he grew, and Ahmed shrank into himself. When the old man planted himself inches away from his grandson's head, Ahmed was the size of a dying baby between his feet.

Ahmed wanted to ask his grandfather for some water to quench his thirst, but he knew it wasn't appropriate for him to talk to grownups. He thought maybe he could baby talk to his grandfather, but he was terrified his grandfather would then treat him like a baby and give him mother's milk, which would leave him even more thirsty. He saw that he was completely at his grandfather's will. He imagined living the rest of his life this size. People would harass him the way young children harassed the only child-sized adult in the freeg. He would have to learn how to have magic ears that filtered out all the negative talk and let in only the positive comments.

The old man undid his leather belt and inserted the tip into the guirbah. He eased the other end between the child's lips and let very tiny drops slide into his mouth. The child wanted to drink all the water at once, but the wise man wouldn't allow that, because his stomach had shrunk so much it would have blown up if he drank like a grownup. The child's tongue was becoming wet and flexible, and he was trying his best to catch the tiny droplets. Most of the water spilled over his face and soaked the clothes around his neck. He could understand that he had become a small baby, but not how his grownup clothes had also shrunk. He felt that his grandfather was spilling the water on him on purpose, because it wasn't only his stomach that was crying for water; his whole body and even his clothes were burning, as if on fire.

He felt the coolness of the water all over his body, and he could smell fresh-grown grass after days of rain, mixed with the old urine of his grazing camels. His nostrils and his heart opened so wide he could breathe like a camel and be happy as a squirrel. The tiny drops his grandfather was giving him just one at a time were blowing life back into every inch of his frail body. And then the guirbah was empty, and the old man disappeared with it, without a trace.

Ahmed was slowly starting to feel his hands and feet. A new kind of tingle ran down his spine. The heat burning him alive was gone, replaced by something that was neither too cold nor too hot, a mysterious warm feeling.

A group of people was talking in a tongue that he couldn't quite understand, and he turned his head toward them. The music and pace of their speech were the same as back home, and he could pick up one word and then another. The smell of well-brewed green tea filled his nose, allowing even more fresh air into his hungry lungs. He could hear the tea being poured continuously not far from where he lay. The chatter, the tapping of the glasses, and the pouring from one cup to the other and back into the teapot made a beautiful music of its own. Far off, he could hear the cries of children. A woman was shouting to her child. A muezzin called to prayer. His voice was hoarse, but comforting and mellow. The grumbling of camels and mooing of cows filled the air of the falling night.

A little girl with a white smile and a ponytail coming undone handed him a half-full cup of tea, the rest of the cup filled with foam. Her skin was as brown as the color itself, which made her white teeth stand out even more. If pure innocence had a name, it would be her name. The tea was dark red and the cup was surprisingly clean, unlike the kinds of cups he was used to back home. There it was impossible to keep the desert out of the glass, so Ahmed was used to tea mixed with sugar and many grains of sand. But the people here, wherever he was now, used fresh mint instead of sand grains. The minty tea settled in his head, awakening all his deep-seated good memories.

He tossed the empty cup toward a thick and beautiful woman whose veil framed her brown, slightly curly, freshly braided hair. She caught it with the reflexes of a wildcat. She said nothing, but her studying look seemed to acknowledge and approve of his quick recovery. He felt fit and full of life, even stronger than before his ordeal. There was nothing he couldn't do, and nothing that could do him harm. But he didn't know where he was, or why or how.

Outside the tent he saw a clear stream running through a high-walled canyon, lined with lush green grass and towering palm trees laden with ripe dates, so many that if not for their thick and steady trunks the trees would have given way. Camels, cows, and donkeys were lying and bathing in the fine sand beside the stream. This place was a piece of heaven, one of those secret oases from legends that had been saving desperate people and caravans for hundreds of years, a station of salvation in the middle of the desert for a lucky few who survived long enough to find their way to it.

A muscular man sat next to him, wearing an indigo turban that covered everything but a band around his big sparkling eyes. His turban and matching boubou painted the skin around his eyes a mysterious dark blue. He exuded an authority that marked him as the man of the tent. "Where's my camel?" Ahmed asked the man. His other questions could wait. Until he spoke, he couldn't be sure he still possessed the faculty of speech at all, and what he needed to know most was whether Laamesh had survived.

The man, and the little girl and the tea-making woman, looked at him, smiling but not saying anything. Ahmed repeated his question in the Berber dialect of Zenaga, again with no response. He tried a version of Tuareg closely related to Zenaga, and could see a hint of recognition. With repetition the man seemed to understand Ahmed enough to answer him. What he said remained almost unintelligible to Ahmed, but he could feel the words. He was in friendly territory.

The little girl extended her tiny fingers to take Ahmed's rough, wounded left hand, evidently untroubled by the missing finger. Ahmed let her guide, following her along the stream. She stopped, still smiling, and pointed to Laamesh grazing on a lush green and fresh acacia, the likes of which he'd seen only during rainy season. Many more grew nearby, clean, beautiful, full, and freshly watered. Ahmed called, and the camel stopped grazing until the man could reach him. Ahmed ran his right hand down the camel's long neck and kissed him on the snout. Laamesh returned the favor by running his snout over his master's head and the back of his neck, down to the middle of his back.

All the while, the girl carefully held Ahmed's left hand, and when he seemed satisfied, she gently led him back toward the end of the settlement. Ahmed was beginning to remember vague details from the last few days. He let loose a flood of questions.

How did I get to this place? And when?

Who brought me here?

Where is my family?

Above all, where is Zarga, the purpose of my journey?

He threw these questions in quick succession at the little girl, like an automatic French rifle. He was using her to think aloud, and did not expect her to understand. The girl kept smiling but said nothing. She dragged the man forward subtly but firmly, gesturing for him to follow her. She was dance-walking like a feather, and even the revived, athletic nomad had trouble keeping up.

23

AS THEY went, he saw that he was in a seminomadic settlement with a little more than a dozen families living in a mixture of tents, shacks, and hay dwellings. The girl led him into an open shack, old but well maintained. An old man sat inside, surrounded with books and notebooks. Wooden slates of different sizes for different grade levels leaned neatly against a big metal box on the west side of the shack. An old inkwell made out of clay lay on the man's right, bristling with wooden sticks that served as pens. Ahmed vividly remembered making ink for such a well, a mixture of water, charcoal, and gum arabic. His grandmother would give him a piece of charcoal and make him rub it on the wall of the inkwell until it vanished into the mix and made it black. The mixture must be exact. The charcoal gives the color, the gum makes it stick on the slates and French paper, and the water provides the balance between the two. He would take the pen and try to write something, and then add more water, gum, or charcoal until he was satisfied with the mix.

The sheikh wore an oversized white boubou and an indigo turban wrapped carelessly around his head and neck. He was singing a text of Ibn Ashir in a low, sweet voice as they entered.

Ahmed felt at home hearing the beautiful prose he'd memorized as a teenager and still mostly remembered. He recognized at once the imam's schooling. The great scholar's book would have taught the old man everything a good Malikite Sunni young man needed to know. From it he'd learned to perform the Five Pillars correctly, at least in theory, since for most people this deep in the desert going to Mecca for Hajj was much too expensive and time-consuming, and too far to walk in the scorching heat. Ibn Ashir also would have taught him the basics of Greek philosophy and logical reasoning, such as the fact that the part is always smaller than its whole.

The little girl sat down facing the imam, her hands palm down on her small thighs, her eyes on her hands to avoid eye contact with the old man. She spoke to him for a while, the man interjecting a couple of times. Ahmed knew the conversation must have been about him, but as usual he didn't understand. He busied himself with reading the titles of the books and the writings on the slates, which represented the last Surat each child in the settlement had memorized of the Holy Quran. Every once in a while he would listen intently, trying to decipher what he could.

The imam closed the book he'd been holding and put aside a pair of old reading glasses, the thick black frame held together with thin wire and old tape. The glasses added to the old man's air of scholarship and self-denial; they spoke of a life spent reading very thick books with very small writing, and a life humbled by seclusion, long prayers, and meditation. Ahmed could almost feel the endless alternation of day and night over so many years of his life.

The imam didn't smile, but he had a very friendly face. He opened an old leather bag and filled the tiny hands of the girl with a mixture of dates and nuts. The girl took off running and dancing the Yemeni into the distance.

"My name is Ag Sharif," the man said to Ahmed in Arabic. "I'm the humble slave of this village. Our Prophet, peace be upon him, had the habit of asking those he met about their names and families. What is your name?" The prefix "Ag" in the imam's name meant that he, and probably the whole settlement, belonged to the Tuareg, the way the "Ould" signaled attachment in Ahmed's culture and "de" in French.

Ahmed told the reverent man his name, avoiding the man's eyes.

"Humans are the children of Allah," the man went on. "We are all brothers and sisters. Our father is Adam, and Adam was made of clay. Our salt caravan found you lying under a tree in far Morocco, half-buried by the wind. They thought you were dead. They dug a grave for you, and they washed you and prayed over you, and as they lowered you into the grave one of the men heard a very weak breath coming out of you. No one believed him. Half of the men said that you should be buried in peace as soon as possible, as our religion prescribes, and the other half asked the group at least to check whether a mistake had been made or whether perhaps the caravan might have witnessed a miracle.

"After a long argument, they decided to give your camel a voice and allow him to break the stalemate. The camel was un-tethered and left to go. Instead of leaving, he knelt beside the grave with his head toward Mecca. This was not only a good omen but a clear sign that he could feel that your soul was still hanging inside your body, ready to leave on a moment's notice. The men hurried to lift you from the grave and were able to re-vive you by slapping you and sprinkling water over your face."

The imam spoke as though reading a book, emphasizing every word as if to give it its independent meaning and identity. Ahmed had the sense the learned man rarely conversed in Arabic. Only foreigners respect grammar; if one speaks a language prop-erly, it's conclusive proof that it isn't his mother tongue. Those who eat up the words and butcher the grammar are obviously the native speakers.

"That was not the only way your camel saved your life," the sheikh said. "The men of the caravan only found you in the first place because they heard his growls and changed their path to investigate." He spoke loudly in Tuareg to a young woman who sat outside knitting, then turned back to Ahmed. "No one will die before his day, but when death knocks at the door, no real doctor, nor a French doctor, nor a caravan, nor any number of men can provide salvation. As the Arab poet put it:

And if death sticks its claws in you, you'll find out that no charm can save you!

I have always lived by this principle, but your story has bolstered my belief even more." He looked straight into Ahmed's eyes, which was not a usual thing, "Praised be Allah and your faithful camel. If it wasn't for your camel, you'd be one more sad story to be added to that rich culture of yours."

Ahmed solemnly nodded in agreement. "May Allah reward your tribe and give them a long and happy life!" He thought for a moment, and then opened his hands imploringly. "Can I meet the man who found me?" he asked.

The wise man looked uncomfortable, but his position as an imam required that he answer honestly. "Sheikh El Weli," he said. He took a loud sip from the dirty tea glass and wiped his lips with the hanging tip of his turban. "It was Sheikh El Weli who insisted on going through the pain of his forefathers, journeying to the Moroccan salt flats as they did," he continued. "The sheikh, who specializes in the knowledge of the unseen, said he was told to do so in a powerful dream. He refused the ways of the French invaders, believing that cars are a clear sign of the looming day of judgment, when iron can talk and the far away becomes near. No one understood him before, but now everybody does. No car could have spotted you, and unlike a camel, a car cannot smell or feel."

The imam took Ahmed's right wrist in his left hand, and with his right he formed Ahmed's fingers into a light fist. "Unfortunately, you cannot see the sheikh. He seeks only the reward of Allah, and no one else. He believes that his good deeds will be canceled if one so much as thanked him. And such good deeds! Only he could say a prayer that would warp the ground and make the return journey from Morocco to Timbuktu not in weeks, but a few days. It's part of the knowledge of the unseen, to which sinners like me have no access." He released Ahmed's hand. "What art thou after?"

"Her name is Zarga. Two and a half years old, dark brown with white spots on her head, belly, and front legs. Bearing our brand, the bent stick and the point." He spoke slowly, not entirely confident of his linguistic ability, and without real emphasis or enthusiasm. He had been a herder all his life, and this was not the kind of place he would look for his camel. Ahmed reluctantly went on to explain his journey and his ordeal with the people-eaters. He didn't want to complain, but rather to inform without leaving out any details, in the proper nomad way.

From time to time the woman who sat outside came in with two fresh cups of thick, sweet, well-brewed green tea. The imam never stopped sifting through his many books and rearranging them as he listened, but Ahmed could see he was struggling to make sense of what he was hearing. He had learned from long experience that his people's Arabic was a thick Moorish dialect that was hard for strangers to understand, even learned men. Their conjugations don't follow what's written in the book, and they use their own tenses to express the past and the future. They overuse filler expressions, like "You've got it!," "Yes," and "It's the truth," and because they cannot pronounce certain sounds of traditional Arabic, they add their own sounds and clicks to the language. Every once in a while, the imam had to stop his guest and ask him what he meant.

The sun was sinking fast, taking away the heat of the day and replacing it with fresh air. The imam stood and fastened his belt around his waist, revealing a bigger gut than was common in the kind of life Ahmed knew. Imams face the challenge of finding the golden mean between studying and tending the community livestock. Tending to the animals means they miss the friends they cherished the most, their books and notes. Studying means they sit, to the advantage of their bellies and the detriment of their health. The wise man addressed the tea-making woman in a low voice that Ahmed couldn't hear, then motioned his visitor to follow him out of the tent.

"I have a surprise for you," he said. He seemed to be smiling now, though Ahmed could not be sure. As he walked he played with a miswak, a tooth-cleaning twig fashioned from local shrubs, twirling it in the side of his mouth like a lollipop. His teeth were exceptionally white, evidence of studious use of a miswak over many years.

"Your ancestors were righteous people," the imam said. "Indeed, I have read about many miracles that manifested themselves at the hand of the father of your clan. He owned a camel that traced back to Kaswa, the she-camel that carried our messenger from Mecca to Medina when he fled persecution."

Ahmed basked in the recognition being bestowed on him for actions he had no part in. He was glad the father of his clan had not done shameful things, though if he had, his host would have left them unsaid.

"He performed Hajj on the back of his holy camel, and when he came back, people crowded around the feet of the animal, kissing them and seeking blessings from the feet that touched the holy ground." The imam's words were measured; they were not his own opinion, but what he had read in his books and in the many desert travelers' notes he'd come across. Ahmed turned his face slightly away to hide the rush of pride that washed over him like a breeze from the west. A real man should be able to contain himself and not let his pain or his happiness be read on his face.

The imam's pace quickened. He wanted to get where he was headed before the sun sank into the Ocean of the Oceans, and he proved much faster and fitter than his body suggested. Ahmed felt shame in his heart for misjudging the man's physical abilities. He wished the silent, judgmental person in his head had been wiser and quieter.

The herd was about half a hundred and well-tended and fed. Though the sun had set, the men could still recognize the individual camels. "Do you know that blessed camel?" said the imam, now smiling unmistakably and pointing to Zarga.

Ahmed fell down on his knees, raising the palms of his joined hands to his face, mumbling prayers that flowed spontaneously, without any thought or effort. He then prostrated himself, leaving clear marks of sand on his forehead, nose, and the palms of his hands. He wanted to throw his arms around the imam, but he couldn't give in to his emotions in front of strangers. He wasn't just representing himself but his whole tribe, especially after his host had paid homage to all its good stories. His behavior, bad or good, would be recounted to the children of his children, shaming them or making them proud. When he was alone, when only the camels could hear him and wouldn't judge him, he would laugh and sing loudly and be as happy as he wanted to be. Ahmed merely looked at the imam, smiled, and thanked him. He prayed to God to reward him and his tribe.

"After we loaded our salt from the beach at Beer Sahel, a man offered her to us for a good price. My men bought her, mainly for meat on the way home, but the men decided she was too noble for that, and should be left to bear."

"I can't thank you enough. It goes without saying that I will pay you as soon as the rice is picked," Ahmed said, knowing the Tuareg were doing him a favor by allowing him to buy back his property.

"We will not ask you for anything, not even the price we have paid. We're glad we could serve Allah and you. He bestowed upon us a great blessing in our small oasis, and Allah forbid we indulge ourselves in the sin of greed by asking what is not ours," said the imam, his voice mixing with the camels' voices and becoming one with the herd's. He insisted Ahmed spend the night with him in his hut. As they walked back to the settlement, in a sign of respect, the imam asked his guest to bless his house, and

Ahmed read the first Surat in his heart and blew air toward the house of the imam.

After a restful night filled with good dreams, Ahmed ate ground wheat with milk and drank tea. For his trip home, the imam gave him a small sack of dates, a sack of salt, and a kilo of the finest grade of tobacco leaves. Ahmed packed the provisions, dividing them evenly on the two sides of the saddle. It was a small load for a camel, which could easily carry more than two hundred pounds over long distances. The last sip of the last cup of tea left a sweet taste in his mouth that would reverberate into eternity.

24

SO IS it true that all's well that ends well? Ahmed couldn't say; deep down he believed that a bad past can't be erased by good events, but good things most certainly make a difference when thrown into the mix.

Ahmed headed home, equipped with the navigational information he had been given by his host and the now-restored wiring of his nomadic brain. The morning breeze was fresh and cool, but Ahmed knew he had a very short window before the heat set in.

With Zarga bound to his neck, Laamesh moved clumsily at first. She was used to traveling with a herd and wasn't tamed to be tethered and led. But the more they rode, the more Laamesh settled into a rhythm, and the safer Zarga felt, the more she let go of her resistance.

The trip between Timbuktu and his people's region of Laaguil passed safely and easily. He spent seven nights between the Tuareg camp and his home, each time with a different tribe. He was welcomed and well tended every night, and never even touched the provisions the imam had given him.

On the final day of the journey, as he neared his people's camp, Ahmed made a short detour to visit the grave of his father. It had been too long since he had stopped there, and it was time to talk to him and let him know the latest news.

The family graveyard was battered beyond recognition by the wind. It did not matter: Ahmed could find his father's grave blindfolded. Every time he came the gravestone lay buried under the sand; every time he dug it up, cleaned it, and stood it back in place.

Ahmed threw the end of Laamesh's tether over a branch on a tree beside the grave. He carefully dug up the stone and removed the dust, making sure the name was legible, as well as the verse he'd chosen to reflect his feeling that a part of his soul had been ripped up by the passing of his father, the man against whom he would measure every other man he met in his life.

> Misfortunes have poured over me and turned my days into
> the darkest of nights.

He kissed the stone, prayed for his father, and put his mouth close to his father's ear. "Thanks to Allah, Zarga will soon be back home. I pray to Allah that we meet again in heaven, after a very long life." To Allah, silently, Ahmed added, "I pray that when I reach home, everyone is well."

Ahmed stood up slowly. As he turned to leave, he saw a fresh grave nearby, a week old at the most. As he bent toward the stone to read it, his head began to spin and a cloud covered his eyes. Was it his son? His wife? His mother? With shaking hands, Ahmed picked up the fresh-engraved stone. The inscription read:

> This is the tomb of the forgiven InshAllah Ahmed Ould
>   Abdallahi
> Died of thirst as a martyr in the search of his camel
> To Allah we belong, and to Allah we return

What a relief! Forgetting for a moment that the pain and grief he'd been spared had been visited instead on his family, Ahmed laughed to think that he was now one of two people in the freeg who had gotten to see their own graves. The other was Messouda, the old seer, who one day stopped breathing and was declared dead and buried, and would have remained that way had not the imam seen in a dream that she wasn't dead and called on the freeg, which rushed to the graveyard in the middle of the night and dug her up alive.

In time Ahmed would learn the full story of his family's grief, a story everyone knows. For weeks the camp had been in mourning, from the moment the family learned of his supposed death from a man from the Sahel, who in turn had received very credible news from salt traders who had found the corpse of a man who had died of thirst in the unconquerable dunes of Beer Sahel. The body was decayed beyond recognition, but the bones and boubou the family received days later could easily have belonged to Ahmed. The family buried them in the cemetery, according to the tradition of our Prophet. They performed the rituals for his departed soul and read the whole Quran to his memory. They raised enough money from friends and neighbors to repay his debts, money most of his creditors had refused to accept, because the tradition is to forgive the departed all their shortcomings and debts in order to ensure them a safe journey to heaven. Lost in grieving, his wife Jamila wore the black malhafa, the modest veil that widows wear for four months and ten days to show respect and loyalty to their husbands. His son Abdallahi had wept for days.

But—oh greatest of miracles!—news had reached Jamila and young Abdallahi that Ahmed had been seen that morning laughing over his own grave, and not only that, he had Laamesh with him, and Zarga, too.

As he neared the camp, the singer of the freeg came out with her group to meet him. She sang him the song welcoming the distinguished warrior, the most beautiful of the tunes he had heard as a child, never imagining it would be sung in his honor. New energy washed over his body, filling his lungs with fresh air, as the sweet tune played.

> Salma and those around her had known
> We could curb fighting horses

But when Ahmed entered the camp and knelt Laamesh to dismount, the soothing sound of the drum took over, and Jamila herself improvised a Tala-al-Badr for him.

The wide moon has risen
From the valley of Wadah,
And we owe it to show gratefulness to heaven
Whenever one calls to Allah,
O you who were sent to us
Coming with a word to be heard,
You have honored the city with your coming.
Welcome! Welcome!

And so Ahmed arrived home a hero. For a while this meant he stood apart: the shock of finding he was still alive was great, and the pain of the community's misplaced grief lingered, and it took many people time to accept him back. The fact that he might have had—no, he almost certainly *had* had—a glimpse of the beyond that gave him special powers, including the power to read people's minds, made many around him very uncomfortable.

For a brief time this awkwardness filled the air even between Ahmed and his family. The first night, as he was pouring the first cup of tea, he and Jamila sat stealing glances at one another and trading shy smiles, trying to penetrate the wall of censorship society imposed on intimate conversations and public affection. They felt strange before one another, each seeking in the other their old spouse. But love is love, and before long the strangeness began to fade, as it would in time for the rest of the freeg, as Ahmed lived as he had always lived, minding his own business, respecting everyone, and filtering out the rest.

After the couple finished the third round of thick, sweet tea, Ahmed stepped outside the tent. The clear sky seemed bluer and wider than ever, except in the east, where the setting sun was painting beautiful colors on an ominous bank of clouds. Across the camp another round of singing was slowly dying.

It was happening already: as with all Bedouin heroes, the people of the freeg were already weaving legends around his trip. Until the day he died, on the rare times Ahmed told his own story, he never talked about his bravery and courage, of course. But even on this first night the storytellers had started filling in the gaps. Already they were likening him to his grandfather and proclaiming that he'd inherited the great man's bravery and reverence. Before long they would be describing a bloody encounter with an army of people-eaters that was supported not by one, but by dozens of demons. In that version, Ahmed defeated all of them with his bare hands and the backing of his dead grandfather.

For the rest of his life Ahmed would hear these stories, with slight embellishments added each time. Pepper and salt never hurt any story, as the Bedouins say, especially when the essential truth of the tale remains untouched and it is recounted around a fire. After all, it is around the fire that stories need to be the most beautiful and intense.

Ahmed would listen, never bothering to confirm or deny anything. He let people talk as they wished, giving free reign to their fantasies. He believed praise and criticism should be received equally and we should be moved by neither; we should be like camels, who go about their daily business regardless of what people say or do.

Glossary

adriss (Hassaniya, from Zenaga). The Hassaniya word for the *Commpihona gileadensis*, a tree common in the Western Sahara. The word also refers to a bucket carved from the adriss tree that is used for milking.

arahhal (Hassaniya, probably borrowed from Zenaga). A harness and saddle for a camel generally ridden by Bedouin women; also used as a storage rack or table inside a tent.

Asr prayer (Arabic). One of five mandatory Islamic prayers. It is performed halfway between noon and sunset.

azan (Arabic). The Muslim call to prayer.

bait (Hassaniya, from Arabic, meaning "chamber"). A leather pouch for carrying a pipe, tobacco, and smoking accessories.

bismillah (Arabic). A Muslim invocation, literally "In the name of Allah," often used to express gratitude.

calife (Arabic). A political and religious leader of an Islamic state.

fatilan (Arabic). Literally, "a thin thread." Much like the man in the moon to Westerners, the word *fatilan* is said to be visible to Bedouins as an inscription on the moon on very clear nights.

freeg (Hassaniya, from Arabic, meaning "team"). A Bedouin community or group of tents.

guirbah (Hassaniya, from the Arabic *qurba*). An animal skin for holding and carrying water.

grigri (also *gris-gris*, origin uncertain, possibly from the Yoruba word *juju*, "fetish"). A talisman or amulet used for protection and good luck. It is often a leather pouch inscribed with traditional verses or folkloric sayings and containing ritual objects. The word can also refer to a person who creates and sells grigri.

Hajj (Arabic). The annual pilgrimage to Mecca, one of the Five Pillars of Islam.

hajjab, hajjaba (from the Arabic verb "to hide" or "to censor"). A traditional healer whose powers and cures are believed to put a wall between a patient and evil spirits and influences. *Hajjab* refers to a male healer, and *hajjaba* a female healer.

harira (Arabic). A rich, thick Moroccan soup.

Hassaniya. The dialect spoken in much of Mauritania. It is an Arabic dialect that incorporates elements of Berber, French, and a number of African languages.

hida (Arabic). A song sung by camel herders to their camels.

hajab (from the Arabic verb "to hide" or "to censor"). When transliterated this way in the text, a charm that provides protection from evil spirits or influences.

Hizb (from Arabic, meaning "part"). The portion of the Quran a faithful Muslim reads daily, equal to one-sixtieth of the full

Quran; in Mauritania it is about ten pages of a standard six-hundred-page edition.

h'sairah (Hassaniya, from Arabic *hasser* or *ssad*). A sitting mat that is woven from straw and thin leather threads.

imam (Arabic). The person who leads prayer for a community.

InshAllah (Arabic). Interjection, literally meaning "If Allah wills it!"

jinni (sing.), **jinn** (plural) (Arabic, from the verb *janna*, "to hide"). Supernatural beings that cannot be seen.

kiblah (Arabic). The direction Muslims face when they pray, which always points to the Kaaba shrine in Mecca.

Laaguil. Part of the Trarza region of Mauritania, an area of the Sahara known for relatively shallow water wells. Ahmed's home.

legzana (Hassaniya). A fortune-telling art in which the fortune-teller inscribes symbols in the sand and interprets them.

Makamat (Hassaniya). A form of poetic writing employed most famously by al-Hariri (1054–1122); this form has a characteristic rhythm.

Malikite. Belonging to one of the four schools of Islamic jurisprudence.

miswak (Arabic). A twig used as a toothbrush, common across the Islamic world.

mrah (Hassaniya). The area in or near a nomadic camp where camels are kept for the night.

Sahliya (Hassaniya, from *sahel*, "coast"). The wind that sweeps eastward from the Atlantic across the Sahara.

salam alaikum (Arabic). A variation of the traditional Muslim greeting *as-salaam alaikum*, meaning "Peace be upon you."

Shahada (Arabic). The Islamic creed or profession of faith: "There is no god but Allah, and Mohamed is the messenger of Allah."

shikwah (Arabic). A small animal skin used to store milk and water and to make buttermilk.

Subuh (Hassaniya). Another name for *fajr,* the Islamic dawn prayer.

Surat (Hassaniya). Variation of "sura," a chapter of the Quran.

Tayammum (Arabic). Ritual purification using sand.

titarek (Arabic). A plant or shrub (*Leptadenia reticulata*) used for a variety of medicinal purposes in many parts of Africa, the Middle East, and the Indian subcontinent.

zakat (Arabic). Alms given in charity.

zrig (Arabic). Buttermilk mixed with water and sugar or with water and salt.

Note on Sources

In the text, Ahmed recites from memory a number of passages from the Quran, from classic Arabic literature, and from folklore and oral traditions. I am indebted to Quran.com, which guided my translations of the Quran. All other translations are my own.

—*Mohamedou Ould Slahi*